Books by James Litherland

The *Slowpocalypse* Series

Certain Hypothetical
Threat Multiplication

The *Watchbearers* Series

Millennium Crash
Centenary Separation

For more information, please visit
www.OutpostStories.com

CERTAIN

HYPOTHETICAL

DEDICATION

To God be the Glory

(and all criticism should go to the author.)

CERTAIN

HYPOTHETICAL

JAMES LITHERLAND

Outpost Stories

Disclaimer: As should be obvious, this book is a complete work of fiction. Any resemblance to real persons, places or things is entirely coincidental.

Cover design by James Litherland

Acknowledgments

To my parents for all their love and support,

And to all the dear saints (some of whom have already been called home) whose prayers have helped carry me through.

Contents

Prologue

Pushing the Button

8:45 p.m. Friday, November 22nd

ANTHONY stood behind a cedar, in the shadows beyond the glare of the floodlights, knowing that he could stroll right up to the guards and pass through the gate without question—yet he intended to risk his neck breaking in.

He watched those guards for a few minutes as they inspected the occupants of each queued up and idling vehicle before waving them through into the compound. Even with the later curfew for Friday nights, the line of returning residents in their cars and trucks stretched down the road.

Everyone sat quiet and well behaved, aware that any disruption would delay the checks and that the guards were sticklers who would close and lock the gates at nine p.m. on the dot—no matter how many still waited. And yet, most people came back at the latest possible hour.

Anthony wondered if any of them would end up shut out of the community tonight—it happened— and if in this instance the result would be more unpleasant than usual. *They still might be better off than those of us inside.*

He admitted to himself that he was tempted to walk right in. He was physically exhausted, and the urgent information he possessed weighed heavily on his mind. But what seemed easy enough right now would only cause difficulties in the future. He had slipped out of the compound this morning without anyone knowing, and if he were to be logged back in without having been logged out in the first place, eventually there would be questions.

Questions and consequences. Anthony found his jaw had clenched as his thoughts turned to what might come of his actions this day. He sighed under his breath and banished the distracting speculation. Keeping his tread light, he backed across the carpet of fallen leaves and needles, stepping farther into the forest.

He started by skirting the security fence. The whispering breeze covered the sound of his passage, and the shadows of swaying branches hid his own fleeting figure. Anthony circled the compound for almost four miles before coming to the large oak standing not fifteen yards from the fence.

He lifted the underside of his left wrist in front of his face and gently rubbed it with his right thumb until the time started to glow softly under the skin. *Plenty of time.* He had memorized the schedule for the perimeter patrols—another strict routine that never varied and a flaw in their security measures that needed to be fixed.

After he had exploited it.

There were no low-hanging branches, but Anthony had climbed his share of trees—though he dreaded the effect on his clothes. *Sacrifices have to be made.* He unzipped one of his jacket pockets, pulled out his thick, ridged gloves and tugged them on and scurried up the trunk to a large, sturdy limb. Twenty feet above the ground he rested.

Standing roughly as high as the top of the fence itself, he reached his left hand up to steady himself with the branch above and walked out to where he could look over the perimeter wall and see the back of the Learning Labs Annex.

He grinned. The building and those around it stood closed and dim. On a Friday evening chances were slim anyone would be about in this area. From this distance at least, he couldn't make out any people—and as long as he wasn't observed entering the compound in such an unorthodox manner, he'd be able to maintain the fiction that he'd never left.

Anthony looked down at the branch beneath his feet. It seemed sturdy enough where he stood now, but the tree limb thinned as it stretched toward the top of the fence. Of course it had been trimmed to prevent it from extending too close, but even before the branch ended it would fail to support his weight. He took a few cautious steps further out on the limb and tested to see how much give there was—tested gently.

It would be difficult. Anthony calculated in his head—not with actual numbers, but with the intuition he'd developed from long experience. He saw how much momentum he'd need at the point where he'd have to jump. He saw just how he would have to place his feet, and how much spring the giving branch would supply. One small error alone could put him on the ground with a broken back, or enmeshed in the razor wire on top of the fence. Either scenario was unpleasant.

Anthony worried what would happen if he were to fail to deliver his report in time and felt the weight of responsibility settling upon his shoulders. Then he took a deep breath and just let it go. He wasn't in control. The fate of the world didn't depend on him, however much he might feel that way. He couldn't begin to fathom all of the potential consequences of his actions. He could only do what felt right deep down in his spirit—and trust.

Anthony checked the time again. Soon enough the regular patrol would come through, examining the buffer zone between fence and wall. He let his hand glide back up to the higher branch and held himself still while he waited. A little movement of the branches would seem the work of the wind and likely wouldn't even register with the guards, but a sharp rustle might attract their attention. And Anthony's current position would not withstand any scrutiny.

After several minutes the two-man patrol appeared, casting casual glances left and right as they marched along. *Very sloppy.* Like the gate guards, they were rigid in their discipline but lax in their duty. Anthony used the interval while he waited to breathe slow and deep, gathering his energy.

Once the distraction of their presence was gone, he again ran his mind over just how his body would need to perform to make it cleanly over the fence. Then he considered how he needed his body to hit the ground to avoid doing himself serious injury. Which he would if he didn't land properly.

He calmed his nerves. This was the time for allowing his instinct and experience to take over. He focused his mind on precisely what he meant to do as he cycled through a few more deep breaths. And when his spirit was ready, Anthony pounded a few powerful strides down the length of the branch and launched himself through the air.

He stretched his hands out in front of him as if he were diving into a pool—a pool twenty feet above the ground, with the water's surface facing him in the air. He imagined himself striking that surface above the razor wire. Then his body curved downward and he focused on the approaching ground as it really was so he could meet it at a glancing blow.

He folded his hands inward as he impacted, not taking the brunt of the force but subtly altering his trajectory as he tucked into a roll. He kept rolling, transferring his energy into forward momentum. He tumbled across the ground most of the way to the perimeter wall before enough of his kinetic energy had dissipated to allow propelling himself up into a standing crouch.

Anthony grinned even as he winced. He stood with care and stretched his muscles as he took stock of his condition. He knew he'd be sore, but miraculously he had not broken, sprained, or even pulled anything. The perimeter wall still loomed ahead of him. Thankfully, it was only ten feet high and the iron spikes on top were merely decorative. They'd make good handholds.

Anthony allowed himself another few minutes rest. Although the next part should be simple, his strength was starting to ebb. Finally he took a deep breath and a few steps backward. Then a short run and he was scrambling up the wall and grabbing the wrought iron to hold his head just over the top while he looked for signs of life on the other side.

Satisfied the entire area remained empty, Anthony heaved himself over with care and dropped down gently. He'd jostled his insides enough. He walked toward the back of the building, glancing around to confirm as best he could that he hadn't been seen. Then he turned and drifted around the side to the front, casting his eye over the doors and windows. Now he was just doing his job. Now he had an acceptable answer if anyone questioned his behavior.

He looked down at the dirt and grass stains on his clothes, and the sight caused him physical pain. It wouldn't be hard to come up with an explanation, but he'd prefer to get to his quarters without being seen in such a dilapidated state. Miles would have to wait as Anthony took time to make himself presentable.

So he weaved his way between the empty halls, hemmed around the back playfield to avoid the student dormitories, and strode past the front of the Ag Center. Then he circled around to the back door of Security Headquarters hoping to avoid his staff. At least until he'd managed to change clothes.

Anthony removed his FURCS pad from its hiding place in the wall and inserted his security key. He opened the heavy door just enough to slip inside and took two long strides down the hall and into his darkened office by the side entrance. That brief trip had afforded a glimpse of an officer at the duty desk but no one else.

Thankfully, Anthony knew his office space like the back of his hand and was able to strip and put on one of his spare uniforms without injuring himself. He stuffed his abused apparel in the bottom drawer of a filing cabinet before turning on the lights. And then dashed to the mirror to examine himself.

Dirt smudged his face and forehead, and a few blades of grass hung in his hair. He grabbed a hand towel from one of his desk drawers and a water bottle, which he upended to soak the towel. Which he then used to wash his face and hands. He raked his wet fingers through his hair and checked the mirror again. He still looked a little ragged, but it was good enough. It would have to be.

He waltzed out his office's front door and appeared right behind Officer Courdray. She whirled in her chair to stare at him. "I didn't think you were in, sir." But she made the statement a question.

Anthony smiled wide. "It's alright, Lisa. I was just grabbing myself a catnap." He glanced around the otherwise empty lobby. "Quiet night so far? I imagine that will change. But I'm still off duty. So, don't you dare call me. I'm heading out and I don't want to be disturbed."

"Who's the lucky woman?"

"Officer Courdray—" He tried to scowl at her. "That's nonsense."

She shook her head in sad denial, but Anthony didn't care to dally. He turned on his heel and headed down the side corridor and out of the building to where they stabled their electric carts. Two of the buggies were gone, as they ought to be. He would wager his student volunteers performed their duties with much more diligence than Chief Gray's guards. He slid into one of the remaining carts, backed out, and headed for the Green.

Despite the delays he'd already encountered, he still needed to avoid attracting undue attention this evening. So he decided to enjoy tootling along. It was restful for his mind and body as he glided with care along the wide walkway that outlined the giant circle of perfectly maintained turf, dodging inattentive pedestrians. He made sure to cast stern glances at the picnicking couples—in his uniform, making him the very picture of normality.

Anthony parked his cart by the entrance next to Fielding Hall and walked up to the Admin Building, using his FURCS pad to enter by the staff door and leaving his electronic footprints wherever he went.

Though now that he was back inside the compound it should all appear quite routine. He wasn't naïve enough to try using his pad or the net for anything he wished to keep private from prying eyes.

Anthony took one look at the central stairway and headed straight for the elevator. He used the short ride to the fifth floor to finish composing his thoughts and stepped out into the deserted lobby. He glided around the reception desk to the security door—here he had to plug his security key into his pad, insert the key into the lock and press his thumb against the pad's screen. The door unlocked and he passed through into a brightly lit office suite.

He stopped for a long and lasting sigh. A square of desks in the middle of the space was ringed by an outer row of offices, with the director's rooms in the far corner. Since Miles had been living there lately, Anthony had little doubt he would find the man in. He banged a perfunctory knock to give warning and pushed inside. As he'd suspected, Miles was behind his desk. Awake and at work.

The light shined even stronger here, revealing the creases in Miles' shirt and the dark circles under the man's eyes. Anthony couldn't help thinking the director needed more rest. He pushed that twinge of sympathy to the back of his mind—none of them would be getting much rest. Not now, and not anytime soon.

Anthony settled himself into the soft as butter leather sofa—no need to stand on ceremony when it was just the two of them. He leaned forward to prop his head on his hands as he looked Miles in the eye. "It's worse than we thought, Jon."

The corner of the man's mouth dared to twitch. "I take it you've had a hard day, Anthony?"

"And I'm about to have a difficult night." Anthony rubbed his hands over his face. "I've got a lot to report, so let me get it all out." He went ahead and gave the director a detailed report on his day's activities, with verbatim quotes from his sources. It took nearly an hour to go over everything.

Miles refrained from interrupting, but partway through the story he grabbed his FURCS workpad and started tapping out messages. Apparently a decision had been made.

Anthony finished and added his own comment. "It's not quite what you planned for."

Miles shook his head slowly. "No, indeed. The governor's actions are precipitate, and they leave us with little choice."

Anthony felt his jaw clenching again. "Then you *are* decided."

"What would you have me do? If we don't activate the emergency protocols immediately, what do you imagine will happen tomorrow? And this is one of those hypothetical situations in the charter that gives me the authority. I've summoned Ms. Belue to assist us with the preparations."

Tony scratched his chin. "How much does she know about what's going on?"

"Well, she's thoroughly familiar with all the procedures and policies contained in the charter—she actually wrote most of them. But I've never told her what it all *means*. Still, I doubt she'll be terribly surprised by anything."

"But will she go along with it?"

Miles shot Anthony a look of irritation. "Do you think I'd have made Verity my right hand if I wasn't convinced I could trust her? She'll do what needs to be done." The director cleared his throat and softened his tone. "Speaking of what needs to be done, we're going to have to make some additions to our plans to deal with the new complications."

Complications. Anthony took a deep breath and set aside the subject of Ms. Belue. There were more urgent considerations. "When do you think Roberts made his decision?" He recalled the line of vehicles outside the compound. "Someone will need to examine the visitor logs. Anyone recently arrived will be suspect."

Miles shook his head. "We already know of one mole the governor has had in place for a long time, whom you'll have to keep your eye on. There may be others, so don't limit your investigation."

Miles sighed. "But we have more urgent worries than the threats from enemies within. We dare not move against them until we've dealt with the larger problem—the governor attempting to take over by force."

"With all your preparations, Jon, the protocols weren't designed to protect us against the kind of assault Roberts can launch with the State National Guard at his disposal."

Miles nodded. "There are some pieces in place, though. We couldn't have done more—it would've been obvious, and ruined everything. So now we'll have to use a slow lure."

Anthony thought again about the residents who might have tried and failed to return home tonight. "If we push the button now, we'll be creating certain problems."

"If I push the button, you mean." Miles stopped and removed his glasses to massage his temples. "I value your opinion, Anthony. You know that. And you're right—the way this is all going down makes everything dashed awkward. But." Miles stood up from his chair and came around to the side of his desk. "This represents an existential threat to the project."

Anthony understood. He didn't appreciate the situation, but like Miles he didn't see any other option. "What about the other communities?"

"They'll have to make their own decisions, and they're in an even tougher spot, since they'll have far too many options to consider. The Northwest Complex is the only one that is even ready to go online. Anyway, I sent them a message, but it's delayed so they won't receive it until the morning, and coded. We can't risk tipping our hand."

Anthony did admire his friend's ability to plan ahead. "One last thing. Those additions to the plan you mentioned. I hope you meant you've got some notion how to keep us all alive." Despite his words, Anthony found himself grinning.

Miles essayed a brief smile in return. "An idea, yes, but we can flesh that out later. First we should eat, while we go over each of the steps we *have* to take. If we don't start enacting the emergency protocols now, we might not get the opportunity."

Anthony nodded. The weight had returned to his shoulders, and sleep was distant on the horizon. He started to stand but got waved back down.

Miles smiled at him. "You're exhausted. I'll go make the tea. Before Ms. Belue arrives."

Anthony nodded and gave his friend a long look. "And now it begins. Or ends, as the case may be."

Chapter 1

Everything Changes

6:40 a.m. Saturday, November 23rd

DAVID cradled his hands around the warm steel mug and tried to blink the sleep from his eyes. The first weak efforts of the predawn sun were barely enough to see by as he made his way down the sidewalk toward the perimeter wall. His mind failed to focus, despite the crispness in the air—his thoughts were still and quiet, as empty as everything around him. Then, into that silence, a heavy chain rattled and rusty wheels screeched.

He raised his head in confusion. In the distance he saw the great gleaming white of Ken's pickup, idling on the other side of the high chain-link fence as two guards struggled to pull the gate back.

Blinking slowly, David checked his watch—difficult enough, he found, to get up and ready before the first crack of light, but now his boss was having the compound opened early. No doubt to get a head start on the day's work.

David stopped and took a small sip of his coffee while he waited. He took a long, deep inhalation of the bitter aroma to stimulate his senses and felt his brain finally, slowly, start turning over. He usually had a good fifteen minutes to finish waking up—it was one of the reasons he liked to walk down from his mom's house to meet Ken at the main gate in the first place—but here was his boss already at the curb and leaning across to pop the passenger side door open.

David pulled himself up into the spacious cab, slamming the door shut with a satisfying thunk. He noticed the street remained deserted. Because only Ken would be insane enough to arrive before dawn on a Saturday morning. David swallowed another slug of coffee. *Sweet honey-laden heaven.*

"I know you're a big man, Boss—I mean a person with influence." He didn't want Ken to think he was talking about the man's weight. At six-foot-two it was mostly muscle, but if Ken had some extra flab on his frame, it didn't detract from his intimidating presence. "But do you really have to use it to get the gate opened twenty minutes early?"

Ken merely grunted, his own giant mug forgotten in his hand as he stared into the rearview mirror while the truck continued to idle at the curb. David glanced into the side mirror and noticed the two guards pushing the gate closed again. He stretched up and leaned out the open window to stare as the guards looped the heavy chain through and closed the padlock.

David pulled his head back in and turned to his boss. "Making sure they do a proper job of locking up?" Though he wondered why they would bother, when they'd only have to open back up again in another fifteen minutes or so.

"Enjoy your coffee." Ken took his eyes off the rearview mirror and pulled out his FURCS pad and began logging on to the local network.

David couldn't help but sigh. His boss was an old-timer who refused to accept that the pads could automatically connect to the FURCSnet when they got in range. David decided to use this opportunity to down a significant amount of coffee in a couple of long gulps. He believed he'd need it.

Feeling more alert, he watched his boss slip the pad away, shift his bulky frame in the seat, and return his gaze to the rearview mirror. David looked out and back again—in time to see two more guards arrive. The first two had retreated to one side of the perimeter wall and started to slide a tall and heavy-looking iron gate from inside the wall and across the road toward the other side. Together they pushed the thing far inside the opposite wall until it locked into something with an ominous clang.

David hadn't seen that particular gate before or even known it was there. Of course he'd only been living in the community a few months, so the whole business might not be *that* unusual. He tried to get Ken's attention. "What's going on?"

His boss simply shrugged and put the truck into drive. They glided up the deserted central avenue as brighter light began to fan across the sky. Ken started gulping his own coffee as he cast a discerning eye over the roofs and foundations, gutters and lawns of the homes on either side of the street. David might have done the same if he'd been fully awake.

Instead of the usual running commentary about problems needing to be fixed and work to be done, his boss continued to drive in silence, turning down one of the residential streets to continue the casual inspection. As they passed by the Belue home, Ken asked the question. "Why don't you let me pick you up at your mom's house? Or the student dorms, if that's more convenient?"

David shook his head. "Thanks, but this works fine for me."

Ken grunted. "At least you get to spend some time with your mother now."

"Sunday dinners, mostly." David had first met his boss when David had been living with his aunt and uncle on the Gulf Coast. "She's been too busy otherwise." Of course, he was quite busy himself, between work and classes and what little social life he managed to eke out. He didn't blame his mom.

David took another slug of coffee before turning to business. He pulled out his own FURCS pad and called up the queue of complaints and requests to be dealt with. Ken had drilled the priorities into him. David could now sort all the routine tasks from the urgent problems. Before he could finish, though, a new message came through the business filter. An administrative alert. A quick glance at the content forced an unintended groan from his throat.

David turned to his boss and saw he had Ken's attention. "You've been summoned by the deputy director." Also known as David's mother.

His boss frowned but said nothing, just slowly pulled a U-turn and headed back toward the main thoroughfare, which led straight to Admin. Something was in the wind. Between the behavior of the gate guards and this, David could see that much, but he couldn't imagine what it might be.

He wasn't surprised that his mother had official business with Ken. Indeed, it was inevitable. Yet he'd never before had an occasion to visit her workplace, and now he'd see it first in his capacity as a part-time gopher. Somehow David felt faintly embarrassed, and that did surprise him.

His boss swung the truck into the restricted lot by the main entrance and parked it right in front of those doors and started to slide out of the pickup. He paused with one foot on the ground and jerked his head at David, who would rather have waited in the truck finishing his coffee.

Ken had swept inside and made straight for the stairs by the time David caught up to him. Casting a longing glance at the elevator, David hurried up the steep steps, chasing after his boss as he tried to tamp down the apprehension rising in his gut.

As they emerged onto the fifth floor, David had managed to squelch his stomach if not his curiosity. He wondered what connected Ken with his mother and that business at the gate. If he kept his mouth shut and just listened, maybe he could piece enough together to figure out what was happening.

A reception desk sat empty, the door behind it standing open onto a large suite of offices, where a swarm of people buzzed around in a frenzy of activity. David knew his mother often worked Saturdays, but he hadn't expected the place to be this busy.

Four desks formed a square in the center of the room, and in the middle of that space sat the only person David could recognize. Toby was a bean bag with thick glasses and fine brown hair in a bowl cut

—and according to David's mother the man was a competent dynamo. Toby was her valued assistant and gatekeeper. And right now Toby looked to be occupied with four or five different tasks.

Ken walked on in, pausing only to nod at David to stay behind, then strode to the far side, barging into the office opposite. David caught a glimpse of his mother's face as she raised her head, before the closing door cut off his view. At least he was spared witness to that confrontation.

He flashed a grin at Toby and let his eyes roam, but he saw nothing to indicate what it was that had everyone working so hard. So he gave up wondering for the moment and tried to just wait.

Toby flashed him a return smile, but none of the others paid David any attention at all—they flew around him like he was a piece of furniture. David eased closer to Toby's desks to get further out of the general flight path, and waited for an opportunity to speak.

With Toby typing into one workpad while talking into another FURCS pad, it was difficult for David to judge the right moment, but when he noticed the man pause for a second, he interjected a quick comment. "Busy, isn't it?"

Toby stopped. He looked a bit weary, like he might appreciate a break. But he wasn't smiling. "It's serious, alright."

"Is it top secret, or can you give me a hint?"

Toby pursed his lips. "If you'd taken your job here with us, you'd already know all about it."

"Work for my mother?" David couldn't see that being anything but awkward.

Toby shook his head. "Office work would have been more your speed. You're just not the construction type."

David bit back his reply. Everyone saw him as bookish, but he'd labored hard rebuilding homes after Hurricane Ashley. He might not be the 'type' but he could do the work. He didn't mention that, though, as he didn't think Toby would understand his point-of-view. "I get plenty of admin as Ken's assistant. Anyway, it's just part-time. You know I'm studying to be a lawyer?"

Toby ought to appreciate that, and the man did unbend a little. "There's been some kind of threat— the nature of that *is* top secret, for now—so they've put the compound on lockdown. There'll be an official statement soon."

"Lockdown? Isn't that Security's thing?" Since it was early on a Saturday morning and most sensible people were still in bed, David supposed they'd felt no need to rush out an announcement. It could be a while before most people even noticed anything unusual. "All this activity can't be only for making a statement?"

"We've got to cross-reference the resident files with the security logs. To find out who was actually inside the compound when it was sealed this morning and who wasn't, and where they might be so we can—" Toby swiveled in his chair and hit a few keys on his workpad. "Although—"

David boggled a bit. "How long are they expecting this lockdown to last?" But he wouldn't get an answer to his question, as Toby had already plunged back into his work.

No doubt David's mother was explaining everything to Ken right now, and surely his boss would be filling David in before long. Nonetheless, David had nothing else to do but wait, so he took out his pad and checked the news.

There was nothing on the local FURCSnet, but that was no surprise. They were always behind anyway, and surely Admin would delay any story until after an official announcement was made.

The major news outlets would be reporting the threat, though, if it were that big a deal. However, David could find nothing beyond the local network. There was no connection to the outside web at all, and although that *could* happen by accident, he did *not* think that was the case. He imagined either a threat to the network itself, or an attempt to control just how and when residents found out about whatever this threat was. *A news blackout.*

He didn't have much opportunity to speculate, though, about what might've prompted it. His bleak thoughts were interrupted by the door of his mother's office swinging open, with his boss heading for the lobby and barely glancing at David, who hurried after him. Ken made straight for the elevator doors, and waited. When the car arrived, he stepped in and motioned for David to follow.

Entering to stand behind his boss, David examined the man's blank expression and relaxed stance and saw determination. His own mood was relief to be out of that place, and curiosity. Which might not be satisfied for a while yet, but he continued to feel lighter as he trailed Ken back to the truck. Even the man's continued silence didn't bother him.

Still, he considered what approach to take as his boss pulled the pickup out of the parking lot. Better to avoid the subject of his mother. Best to start by offering something, even if it was information Ken already possessed.

"There's been some kind of threat. No idea what though. Didn't hear any more." David let the comment lie there while his boss focused on driving. He expected a response, and eventually it came.

"Threat." Ken blew air out between his lips as if that was a comment in itself. He turned down a side road before continuing. "They're anticipating an all-out assault. So they've sealed everything up tight as a drum. No clue when or how or what kind of attack, but we're to make preparations."

David managed to keep his mouth from hanging open. It sounded bad, even though it didn't really explain anything or make any sense yet. He noticed that Ken had refrained from saying they didn't know who might attack the compound or why, so David figured they knew and that Ken did too. But hadn't said. Since Ken didn't seem inclined to explain further, David figured it would be useless to ask. And even more useless to try to guess.

Then he noticed they had come to an unfamiliar area near the back of the compound. Visualizing the layout of the place, he estimated they must be close to one of the far sections of the perimeter wall. This was a question he *could* ask. "Where are we headed now?"

"Warehouse 6b." Which Ken clearly felt needed elaboration. "We're setting aside the usual maintenance work and starting a new construction project. The supplies we need will be at the warehouse."

By the time he'd explained, they'd arrived. Ken swung the truck to a stop in front of a few short steps leading up to a bare metal door. He sat there for a minute, quiet. "I summoned the crew while I was in with the deputy director."

David found himself nodding. Ken's crew were technically subcontractors, but they worked mostly for Ken's company. Those experts had spearheaded the building of the FURC facilities and community, and they'd settled here once the work was done.

Of course Ken wanted his crew on board for any big new project. But if any of them had been traveling outside the compound, David had no idea what might be involved in bringing them back inside.

"Boss, the whole crew *is* here? On the inside?"

Ken turned and squinted at him. "I made sure they were."

David breathed a sigh of relief, but he remained concerned about the situation. Then he recalled his boss didn't live in the community.

"What about Fiona and the girls?" Ken's family lived on a vast ranch several hours' drive away.

His boss ignored the question. "Come on." Ken left the truck and walked up to the warehouse. David took his time following. He'd had a shock and was still digesting the possible implications. Separated families would only be one.

At the door, his boss plugged a security key into his FURCS pad and used it to unlock the warehouse and enter. David came in behind, walking into the cool, stale air as he heard the fans kicking on. Then the lights popped on and he saw a gigantic space. It remained dim, though. With the lights far up in the rafters, by the time their illumination drifted down to the floor, there wasn't much left.

David could still see enough to take his breath away—boards and cement blocks and long metal rods in dizzying number piled all down the sides of the building, massive shelving that must have been twenty feet high and packed full of who knew what. And all of this had just been sitting here, waiting. He tried to think what it could build.

He tore himself away from gaping and went to watch Ken plug his FURCS pad into the side of a free-standing counter. The entire thing lit up—it was one big screen displaying inventories and blueprints and other plans. The new project.

Ken sped through dozens of different diagrams. It all whizzed by too fast for David to examine the specs in detail, but he saw enough to grasp the magnitude of the job, the amount of work involved.

"Boss. This calls for extensive modifications to the entire perimeter wall. Eight sections, each nearly three thousand yards—that's over thirteen miles."

Ken nodded as he continued scanning the display. "Remember when we were putting in six ten-hour days every week?"

David's heart sank. What he remembered was foolishly volunteering to help rebuild. He'd learned how far he could actually push himself if he had to, and it had almost killed him. David had fervently hoped he'd never have to endure such an ordeal as that again.

Ken clapped David on the shoulder. "You managed once, you can do it again."

They both turned at the sound of Ken's crew filing in through the open door into the warehouse. Even though Ken saw them all from time to time, the men came in shouting loud greetings and wanting to shake his hand. Ken's crew reunited.

David had spent enough time around them to know they were good men, but they were also big, brawny men who lived in another world, with different interests than David. The exception was Jeffrey—thin and wiry and wearing spectacles with tiny frames, he didn't look as tough as he really was. And he read books. So David had a special liking for the landscaper.

The crew exchanged updates on how they and their families were doing, laughing together as they got ready to get down to business. The men weren't displaying any unusual curiosity or concern though. David presumed Ken must not yet have mentioned the trouble that was brewing.

Steve was the first to ask. "So what's this great big job you've got for us?"

Ken glanced around to make sure they were all listening. "A major overhaul to the perimeter wall. New security measures, installing other upgrades to the compound's defensive capabilities." He reached up a hand to scrub the graying bristles on the top of his head. "They'll make a big announcement later this morning. Governor Roberts may try to take this place by force."

Ken's crew were stunned into silence, so David asked the next question. "Why?"

His boss coughed into his hand. "Florida's seceding. Roberts is claiming this whole place, *all* the federal property in the state." He looked around at them all. "Who knows what that nincompoop might do to try and enforce that claim? So we start getting ready for the possibilities."

Steve spoke up again. "We'll need to bring in a lot of workers."

Ken shook his head. "The compound has been sealed, to prevent the governor's people from just waltzing in and taking over. We'll have to make do with the ones already here. And we'll be drafting in some help from the community." He coughed again and turned to look at David. "During this emergency, regular FURC classes have been suspended. The director will be asking every student to pitch in by working full-time."

David found himself nodding. "You did say ten-hour days. *I* wouldn't have had time for my classes anyway, but I don't know how much help a bunch of student volunteers will be."

Ken's crew shuffled around as everyone chewed over the news. David didn't know what *they* were thinking, but he was wondering how on earth the political situation could have played out to produce such a preposterous result. He was also amazed at how well his boss had moderated his language. The circumstances called for a lot more swearing.

Ken hadn't finished, though. "It won't be easy. Getting the work done as fast as we can, since we don't know when anything might happen. Making sure the job's done right, with a bunch of inexperienced workers." He looked at David again. "But we've managed before."

David stared his boss straight in the eye as he thought about the whole warehouse full of supplies and the monumental task ahead of them. "So where do we start?"

"Over at Admin they're busy going through the files to see who they might pull off of non-essential jobs and assign to this one. Then Monday morning we should get those folks, and some student volunteers. But for today, we can plan out the work ahead and do up some rough schedules."

Ken pulled Steve and a couple of the others over to start looking at the blueprints. Then he nodded at David and Jeffrey to follow him over to a great pile of boxes—stacks of small, thin containers marked only with serial numbers.

Ken reached out for one and handed it to David. "One of the most important jobs to be done will be planting these motion detectors. The security fence isn't much of a barrier, so these sensors need to be installed along the entire buffer zone between the fence and the wall. Knowing when and where an enemy comes through will be vital intelligence."

David opened the box to reveal a sophisticated device that somewhat resembled a landmine.

"That's sensitive equipment, so be careful how you handle them. I'm only going to show Jeffrey and you how to set them." Ken addressed the landscaper, "The sod will have to be cut and replaced so as to be invisible. I'll rely on your expertise for that."

He looked back at David. "I'm going to take the rest of the crew, and all the experienced workers we manage to scrounge up, for working on the wall. I'll send the student volunteers out to you in the buffer zone."

David glanced over at Jeffrey, who was now examining one of the motion detectors. "Just the two of us? And some students who've likely never done any manual labor? Will it even be safe to work outside the wall?"

"Colonel Gray will assign a guard detail to protect your crew." Ken frowned. "But I'll be needing Jeffrey's experience for more than just planting the sensors. Still, he'll be around enough to make sure everything's going smoothly. And fix anything that needs fixing."

Jeffrey pushed his glasses back up his nose and winced. "Well, at least it will make a change from continually repairing the Green from the depredations of those young people." He cleared his throat and glanced at David. "Though I'll probably still be cleaning up after them."

David himself wondered how much help his fellow students would actually be. He'd likely end up doing more than his share of the work, but he didn't mind pulling most of the weight. As long as the job got done. He didn't envy Jeffrey the job of trying to corral them, though, especially if the man couldn't be around all the time to supervise.

Ken had been having a quick word with the rest of the crew, and now he stepped back over to them. "They want us to save gas for if and when, so we're getting three of the large electric carts, the kind they use to pull the tram cars. We can use them to haul equipment and personnel back and forth. You'll get one for the buffer zone." He faced David. "You're getting promoted. It'll be your work crew, and your responsibility to supervise the student recruits."

David opened his mouth to protest, but he knew it was futile to argue with Ken once the decision had been made. He'd just have to do the best he could.

Chapter 2

Almost Everything

10:05 a.m. Saturday, November 23rd

KAT skipped down the wide marble stairs two at a time, bounding across the landing and out of the dormitory with a curt nod to a couple of girls she recognized. She pulled a scrunchie from her jeans pocket and bound up her hair as she power-walked across the lawn in front of the Student Center. *Late again.*

She smiled to herself as she breezed through the main entrance, into the Media Centre. She'd get a pass on the jeans and t-shirt, but Caroline would have a fit to see Kat show up without makeup. Kat would have grabbed her baseball cap if she hadn't been in such a rush, just to complete the outrage.

Back in the production area, the staff darted up and down the halls in every direction, like fish with predators on all sides. They parted around Kat as she slid through them to reach Caroline's dressing room. After a peremptory knock, she slipped inside. There Stacy the hairdresser was sculpting the massive mane of red curls belonging to the beautiful but middle-aged actress.

Kat focused on the reflection in the mirror, and blurted out her usual greeting. "So—are you ready to fire me yet, Caroline?" She was paying close attention and noticed only an eyebrow twitch.

"You should let Stacy do your hair, dear. Of course it's gorgeous, but if you don't do something with it, no one will notice." Caroline lifted her eyes to look at Stacy in the mirror. "I'm sure Stacy would adore working on you, wouldn't you, love?"

The small brunette standing behind Caroline's chair nodded silently as she continued her work, likely because people who disagreed with Caroline didn't continue working for her. Kat herself being the sole and unfortunate exception.

"This isn't working out."

Caroline tried to shake her head, but Stacy held it firm. "Nonsense, Katherine. This will work out perfectly. You just have to give it time."

Kat thought 'perfect' was the last word to describe the current situation, but she refrained from saying so. She'd placed limits on her rebellion and was wary of crossing the lines she had set herself. "This job doesn't suit me."

Caroline opened her mouth in mock surprise. "And working as a campus cop did?"

"Safety aide," Kat corrected, "and I worked *with* the security officers."

"A dangerous job, mixing with low characters."

Kat grinned. "At least I got to wear a stylish teal baseball cap as part of the uniform." Her grin faded. "And those 'low characters' of yours are my friends and classmates." As for danger, most of the job had been clerical work. At least she'd gotten to escort lone travelers across the compound at night, even if she'd had to drive around in one of those little electric carts.

"They may be your fellow students, but most of them are certainly not in your class. Besides, you're a sophomore now."

Kat thought the first unwarranted and the second irrelevant. She began to heave an ostentatious sigh but caught herself in time. She wondered if histrionic overacting could be contagious, then worried that it might be genetic.

"There are better ways to bond, if that's truly what you want, Mother."

Stacy let slip a startled gasp, and her nimble fingers paused for a second. Caroline's mouth was a hard line. "Nonsense, Katherine. I feel like I know you so much better already. And it's clear there's a lot I can, and should, be teaching you. Manners, for one thing."

Kat turned on the spot and headed for the door.

"Where do you think you're going?" Caroline snapped. "This is an important broadcast. I need your help."

Kat looked back over her shoulder. "I'm getting breakfast—I haven't had anything to eat yet. And every show is vital to you. It'll be fine."

Caroline shot her daughter a strange look in the mirror, but Kat breezed on out the door before her mother could reply. She zipped down the corridor to the staff café, where there seemed to be more frayed nerves and fewer smiles than usual, likely because Caroline's programme started in less than an hour. These people knew they were supposed to look harried even when they were enjoying themselves.

Kat frowned as she hopped into line. Working as an intern for her mother should have been easy, but she'd found dealing with Caroline to be a difficult, on-going battle of wills. Perhaps she could yet find a way to weasel out of this.

She gave her order and picked up her meal, all the while trying to imagine a way to get herself fired that she could live with. Her stomach wanted her to focus on food, though. Since digestion and dealing with her mother really didn't mix well, Kat turned her mind to anticipating her breakfast.

By the time she'd made it back to her mother's dressing room, Stacy was gone. And Caroline had swiveled in her chair to face the door, smiling like a cat as it watched a trout flop around on the ground. "Now we're alone, dear, and can talk freely."

Kat plopped down on the vinyl love seat that had been shoved up against the side wall, and displayed her trophies. She sat the quart of chocolate milk between her thighs and slowly unwrapped the giant cheeseburger dripping with fat. She stared at her mother, waiting for comment as she took her first bite. She was used to overwrought expressions of disgust, anguish, and even outright horror.

But Caroline simply smirked. "I suppose you slept late, then flew over here like a whirlwind. Not bothering to start your day like a decent person."

Kat knew her mother meant frittering away the entire morning lounging around and gossiping with her friends. That was her mother's idea of manners. To show her mother she had manners of her own, Kat waited until she had swallowed before responding. "I don't like to waste time." And she returned to devouring her food.

"You could spend some time attending to your appearance, to present yourself better before going out in public. That wouldn't be a waste." Caroline paused while she watched the last remnants of Kat's burger disappear. "I'd wager you don't even check your messages in the morning. You should take the time to wish your friends a good day, find out what's going on with them. Then you might've heard about the big announcement."

"Big announcement?" Kat began gulping down her chocolate milk, hoping her mother was enjoying the performance.

"The days of enjoying your beef habit may be coming to an end, dear." After which cryptic comment, Caroline resumed watching her daughter as the milk went the way of the burger. "I'm not sure about the chocolate."

Kat heard the note of concern in her mother's voice, and presumed Caroline's prejudice against cows didn't extend to the lowly cocoa bean. "What are you talking about?"

Caroline just shook her head. "Anyway, if you don't like it, you can blame your father. I do."

"What are you blaming Dad for now?" Caroline held her husband responsible for an awful lot.

"For completely sealing off the entire FURCS compound indefinitely, of course. That includes no deliveries. So where will the beef and the chocolate come from?"

Kat found herself sitting there with greasy lips trying to imagine just what her mother thought she was talking about. "An announcement, you said. I suppose he gave reasons for whatever he's doing." *Sealing the compound?* "Is it just the beef and chocolate I should be concerned about?"

Caroline smoothed her dress as she stood up from the chair. "Wipe your face so you can escort me to the studio." Then she grabbed her clutch and extracted a moist towelette and handed it over.

Kat snatched the wipe and cleaned up both herself and the remains of her breakfast, and in only a fraction of the time it would have taken her mother. Bounding to her feet, she positioned herself near the door. Ready and waiting. "Reasons, Mother?"

Caroline was checking her makeup one last time in the mirror. "Oh, that Governor Roberts claimed possession of the FURC. For the State of Florida." Apparently satisfied with her appearance, for now, Kat's mother continued, "So Miles closed the place tight. To keep the man—or whomever he sends to take over—from just strolling right in."

Kat opened the door and preceded her mother into the hallway, clearing a space so that Caroline could exit unmolested. "Mother," she started, and then remembered they were in public now, "Caroline, this is federal property. How can the governor claim it?"

"He says he doesn't recognize the authority of the federal government anymore. And considering the way things have been going in Washington, you can hardly blame the man."

Kat continued to run interference as her mother glided across the corridor toward the set. She had a queasy feeling in her stomach—and it wasn't the cheeseburger, her insides loved cheeseburgers—it was the gut feeling that her mother was serious. "Are we doing anything about it—other than closing the community?"

Her mother continued to stare straight ahead, eyes turned inward. "Miles looked a trifle peaked when he made the announcement. He can't be getting sufficient rest."

The other intern on duty must have been on the lookout, because she was standing in the hall, holding the door to the studio open. But Kat pushed in front of her mother to bar the way. "You're the one who bullied him out of his home."

Caroline looked around to made sure the other intern was the only person nearby. Still she lowered her voice to a harsh whisper. "When I decided to move here, I had to live somewhere. I told him he could stay in the house if he wanted, but he insisted this was best. Proper. We *are* separated."

Kat moved aside to allow her mother to sail onto her stage, following her onto the dim studio floor.

Her mother had told the public that she needed to rest from her labors, and had decided to favor the

FURC with her presence. Though Kat had doubted the story. Caroline probably wasn't getting the roles she desired and decided to wait for people to come begging for her to return to the limelight.

Then she had confided to Kat in private the real reason she had come—to get to know her daughter. Kat had believed that even less.

As she stood on the studio floor and waited for someone to bring the lights up, Kat wondered why her parents hadn't just gotten a divorce—and how her mother had gotten her sidetracked.

When the lights came up, she looked around to find Caroline sitting on the plush leather chair from which she presided. Kat stalked over. She meant to drag the conversation back to just what was going on, but her mother saw her coming.

"Miles probably adores camping out in his office." Caroline adjusted her skirt and checked herself on the monitor. "I'm surprised you didn't take your job working over there instead of with those *police*." She tilted her head to examine her daughter. "I wonder why."

Kat thought a better question was why had she allowed herself to be bullied into transferring to this position? Then she recalled there were even better questions that needed to be asked. "So what's being done? How are they going to resolve the situation? How long is this going to continue?"

Caroline waited while the other intern pinned a small mike on the collar of her dress. "For my part, I'm going to try and help everyone adjust. I imagine most people are still in shock, but when they start to realize what it means, naturally they'll be frustrated, upset—angry, even. They need to see I care."

Kat took a few deep breaths. "Angry? Just what is the situation, Mother?"

"Think it through, dear. How many of your fellow students have families out there? How many of the workers? Or how many residents had friends or family members who were traveling over the weekend and are now stranded on the outside?" Caroline checked herself on the monitor again and waved for the intern to come back. "Until this preposterous situation is resolved, fuses will be short. So we'll all have to 'pull together' to get through this. Or anyway, that's what your father said."

Kat watched the girl scurry up to hand Caroline a mirror and a small makeup case, then fade back a few steps and hover. She wondered why everyone saw her mother as sympathetic and caring. Whatever it was, Kat couldn't see it.

What Kat *could* see was a dire situation. Probably even worse than it sounded, if she'd been able to pry more details out of her mother. *Poor father.* No doubt her dad would be the one to take the brunt of the fallout.

Kat waited until Caroline had made her repairs and handed her kit back to the intern. "Then I expect there's a lot of work to be done, Mother. And sacrifices to be made. By everyone."

"Indeed." Caroline nodded. "Regular classes have been suspended, though there's the suggestion that students and teachers can get together on an ad hoc basis. But everyone has been asked to work full-time to help out during the crisis."

Kat saw her opportunity. "If things are that bad, they probably need me back at Security."

Caroline shook her head. "I'll pull some strings to get you assigned here full-time. As my assistant." She smiled at her daughter. "You can help me take the pulse of the people."

"That's a good line, Mother." Kat had to take a stand now, before this got any worse. "But I'm not going to work here, for you. I can be a lot more use somewhere else. Security will be happy to have me back. I still have the cap."

Caroline looked ready to swoon, but it was an act. "We haven't had enough time together, darling. After I sacrificed my career to come here, for you." She looked around the studio as if searching for aid, then turned wide, pleading eyes back to her daughter. "And I do need you. You *can* be useful here. At least say you'll consider continuing here part-time? It's your choice, of course."

"Choice?" Kat tried to absorb the idea that her mother was admitting she was free to choose—after maneuvering her into this position to begin with. "Working here as little as I do is already more than enough for me." Kat looked at her mom for a long moment. Then she made her decision. And heaved an ostentatious sigh. "Alright, I'll continue on here, part-time, for now."

Caroline turned on her cream-on-her-whiskers smile. "Darling." Then her chin lifted a little, and she gazed across the studio.

By now a few more technicians had wandered in to tinker, and Caroline's secretary had entered with the producer to go over some papers. The place had begun to bustle. None of that was what had attracted Caroline's attention, though.

Kat followed her mother's line of sight. Striding toward them was a tall, dashing figure with thick black hair and a slightly Latin look. Tony.

As he approached, Caroline adjusted her skirt again and favored him with the full, gleaming white version of her smile. "Speak of the handsome devil," her mother quipped, batting her eyelashes.

Tony grinned at both of them. "Care, have you and Kat been talking about me?"

"No," Kat said right away, stepping on any response her mother might make. She knew Tony had a reputation as a Romeo—it was unfounded, but she didn't want to encourage him. She realized she was pressing her lips together and willed herself to relax. "We were only discussing how I should be returning to Security. Under the circumstances."

Tony rubbed his chin while he stared into space. "You understand things will be different now, more difficult." He looked at Kat. "We'd love to have you back, of course. But it's your choice."

There was that word again. Kat looked Tony in the eye and gave him a slow nod she knew he would understand. She had what she wanted.

Tony shifted back to Caroline. "You look rested." Kat heard something beneath those words, but she didn't catch the meaning.

Caroline gave him a level look. "I slept. Unlike you and Miles."

Tony grinned. "Do I look like I need sleep?" He held out his arms to show them both how sharp he was dressed.

Caroline smiled at him again. "I wish Miles had learned *something* about fashion from you. That man can make the finest suit look rumpled just by wearing it."

"Care, you're just frustrated because you could never make Miles do anything he didn't want to do." Then Tony became serious. "The reason I came."

Kat noticed that everyone in the studio seemed to have gone quiet and drifted closer. "Tony—"

He waved her back while staring at her mother. "Since I'm responsible for maintaining order, Caroline, I want to ask you to coordinate with me. Help people stay calm. This is a stressful time for everyone. We need to make sure people understand that everything possible is being done."

Caroline lost her smile. "I don't care to do your job for you. Or the director's job for that matter. I'm not going to parrot the party line, nor will I sugarcoat anything. This community deserves to know the facts, and I'm going to give them the truth. I'm a journalist."

A journalist? Kat's mother was reinventing herself again, and it was ridiculous. Worse, everyone was eavesdropping on the performance—but Caroline loved playing a part.

Tony seemed only partially perturbed. "Look, Care. No one's asking you to peddle propaganda. Just be responsible." *Fat chance.* "Don't get people worked up is all."

Kat couldn't believe Tony was trying this line with her mother. He should have known better. He certainly knew Caroline well enough to understand what could be expected of the woman.

Caroline flashed a glance at her daughter. Turning back to Tony, she batted her eyes. "Then Miles had better hurry up and resolve the situation, before people start getting worked up. It's calm right now, but when everyone starts feeling the reality, they'll get frustrated. We're closed off from the world outside and besieged. People will get scared and angry. Will you blame them?"

Tony looked at her. "Isn't it your responsibility to do something about it?"

"It's Miles' job to take care of the problem, and before he's got a mob with pitchforks and torches coming after him."

Kat realized everybody was looking grim and no wonder. They all remembered the videos of the riots in Miami before the National Guard moved in. And then there had been no more, videos, at least. Kat forced herself not to shiver. Her father and Tony would *not* let that happen here.

Caroline stared straight at Tony as she made her final point. "Tell Miles he won't get a free pass from me. My responsibility is to this community. And if everything does fall apart, he'll have only himself to blame."

Tony locked eyes with her for a long moment. "Just make sure you don't go picking up any pitchforks yourself, Care. Or fan any flames."

Caroline turned to reassess herself on the monitor. *The royal dismissal.* Tony backed away several steps, casting a quick look at Kat. She drifted away from the stage with him, as the rest of the audience dissolved, too. *Show over.*

Tony turned to Kat and whispered a suggestion in her ear. "Let's have a private chat."

She looked around the busy studio for a place of privacy. A far corner looked dim and deserted, with piles of cables strewn over the floor. Kat picked her way through the treacherous footing, confident that Tony wouldn't have any trouble navigating himself to the secluded spot.

When they were where they wouldn't be overheard, Kat studied Tony's face. "You wanted a word, Boss?" She crossed her arms and waited.

Tony sighed and rubbed his hand up and down his face. "Kat, your mother's right. People are going to get scared and angry, and it won't just be difficult out there. It'll be dangerous."

Kat pursed her lips. This wasn't the conversation she had expected. "Do you think I'll flinch at danger?" This was ridiculous. "Tony, you know me better than that."

"Wait." Tony put his hands out. "Hear me out. I do know what you're capable of." He let his hands drop. "That's why I want to make you a full security officer. If you come back."

Kat snorted. "Of course I'm coming back. And I get it, Tony, really I do—promoting me means putting me on the front lines. You worry." She grinned. "But you need me, or you wouldn't have dangled the lure of danger to reel me in."

Tony shook his head. "I only have three trained officers, and that won't be enough. The rest are all student volunteers. Reliable, but—"

Kat cocked her head at him. "You don't think they'll be up to the challenge?"

"Just the opposite, Kat. But they need training, and I think you'd make quite a good teacher." Tony squinted at her. "I've known you since you were a little girl. In many ways you're better trained than my experienced officers."

Kat wasn't sure she cared for the qualification, but Tony should know how well she'd been trained, since he had been the one training her since she *was* that little girl. She felt her heart quicken. A security officer, patrolling the community and taking care of troublemakers—and she'd get to help train the new officers, too.

"I've already promised my mother that I'd continue working here part-time." Kat glanced back across the studio at Caroline. "And I wouldn't put it past her to try and strong arm me into more. I don't think she likes me working for Security."

Tony nodded. "Your mother's definitely a force to be reckoned with. But do you remember the first thing I taught you?"

Kat smiled. "How to fall." She'd learned how to avoid getting hurt. And she'd learned how to turn a disadvantage to her favor.

Tony finally grinned. "You got pretty good at ground fighting. So I trust you can deal with your mother."

"I may even manage to get out of this job altogether." Kat lifted her chin and looked Tony in the eye. "After all, one of your advanced lessons was how to fight in tight corners." She noticed he had to stifle a laugh.

"Okay, when you've finished here, come over to headquarters. We'll do an abbreviated orientation and set you up with a schedule."

"You can count on me, Tony." Kat couldn't stop grinning.

Chapter 3

This is Hardly Working

3:35 p.m. Tuesday, November 26th

DAVID sank back against the wall into the limited shade it offered and took a long drink from his water bottle. He dared not stop for too long. Otherwise his crew would quit working altogether, though he doubted it would make much difference.

Before dawn, when it'd still felt cool, even chilly, he'd shifted the markers to set off the little they'd managed to finish yesterday, and the area he hoped his crew could complete by the end of the day. They had yet to accomplish a third of their goal. Now the day's exertion made the air seem hot, and the sun burned like summer. And in a little over an hour the cart would arrive to take his crew away.

David looked down the wall to his left where the two guards also slumped in the shade, their arms hanging loose and their rifles resting on the ground. He didn't think they'd moved for hours. The sight hardly inspired much confidence his crew would be safe, but complaining to their superior had achieved nothing.

Grimacing, he noticed Sgt. Rossiter had returned and was stalking back and forth between fence and wall beyond the markers, head down as he fiddled with his FURCS pad. Wherever the man had been for the past couple of hours, he could still be credited with a greater level of activity than his subordinates.

David chided himself for having uncharitable thoughts. His own failings frustrated him more than anything, because he knew he was falling behind in the vital work they were doing, not living up to the responsibility he'd been given. But there was no use beating himself up, either. His weary body aching, he forced himself to stand and straighten his shoulders. Taking a deep breath, he stepped forward into the sun as he looked around to see how his own men were doing.

Jeffrey, wearing his big floppy hat, was out near the security fence, squatting down as he adjusted the grass where one of the first sensors had been placed. The landscaper had insisted that he alone examine the finished work. He'd arrived well after lunch and started fixing each individual blade of grass to suit. No wonder the Green always looked so perfect.

They'd planned it so none of the crew would be trampling over completed ground. David's job was to make sure the recruits cut the sod carefully and dug the proper holes, then he would come behind them planting the motion detectors. Jeffrey would follow, fixing what needed to be fixed.

David would've preferred working on his own—he could do the job faster and cleaner than his crew. Especially when they'd only managed to find fifteen students who'd been willing. Most had chosen less demanding options for pitching in.

But when Ken had started them off on Monday morning he'd made his position perfectly clear.

David was a supervisor and needed to spend his time teaching them how to do the job and do it right, instead of barging in to do it himself. Though Jeffrey wouldn't have to spend so much time correcting the volunteers' work if David did it all himself. Or did a better job of showing them how.

He stopped worrying about Jeffrey and tried to assess how his crew was getting along. He spotted Greg, a fellow freshman, attempting to cut sod by smashing at it with his spade. Here, at least, David could do some good. He walked over and rested his hand on Greg's shoulder until Greg ceased his struggle with the soil.

"Here—" David took the spade from him. "It's no good attacking the ground, no matter how frustrated you are." He mimed the way Greg had been using his arms to drive the blade down. "You'll only wear yourself out without accomplishing anything."

David checked to see that Greg was paying close attention. "First, place the blade against the ground where you want to cut the sod, but place it at angle. Like this." As he demonstrated, he saw the tool was getting blunt. He'd have to remember to get the kid a new spade as soon as he finished here.

"Now, see the place at the top of the blade where it's wide like a step. That's exactly how you should think of it." David rested his foot on the hilt of the blade. "You've got more power in your leg muscles than your arms, so you'd get further trying to kick the blade into the ground." David stomped with his heel.

"But you want to make things even easier since you'll be doing this a lot." David tried to grin. "So let gravity do most of the work. Lift your weight up on your left foot, and place your right a little above the back of the spade—just like that—and kick as you shift your weight down on your right, shoving the spade in."

He suited action to words. The blade slid clean through the sod and into the earth beneath. "It may take a bit to get the hang of it, but it's a trick worth learning." David patted Greg on the back and went to look for that new spade.

He started crossing the grass toward the mound of tools and other supplies stacked against the wall. Their base camp. On Saturday, Jeffrey and he had transported the boxes of sensors and other needed equipment to a convenient spot. The crew arrived in the morning and dropped their gear there—and returned for lunch and rest breaks, too, since the food and water tank were at the base camp.

"David!"

David stopped, closing his eyes briefly to pray. That was his Mt. Everest calling. Or perhaps the job was the mountain and Eric the cold, harsh wind. Whatever the correct analogy was, David turned to face it.

"What's the problem, Eric?"

Stan and Jake, two of Eric's friends, stood next to a hole, leaning on their tools, sweating and trying to grin. They'd managed that much better earlier in the day. Eric pointed down at the hole. "Is that deep enough?"

David came and looked, and he would've sighed if he had the energy left. "After you remove the sod layer, you dig down another four inches at least, but no more than six."

Which he'd demonstrated for everyone yesterday when they'd started and repeated this morning for Eric and some of the others. "And you need to make sure the bottom of the hole is level." He figured he'd best repeat that now, and maybe it would take this time. At least they were finally cutting the sod in the right size square.

Eric looked down at the hole for a long moment. "Is that six inches? I can't tell."

Jake snickered. David found himself snatching the hoe out from under the man's chin. He must be getting really tired. He couldn't afford to be short with people who'd volunteered to help, even though their assistance didn't amount to much.

David placed the business end of the hoe down the side of the hole. "Both the spades and the hoes are eight inches long—the metal part." *Best to be clear with this lot.*

"So you can see this hole only comes up about a fourth of that, or about two inches. When it reaches at least halfway, then you can stop and start leveling the bottom." He stopped when he realized he didn't have their full attention. "Look. If you keep digging until the hole comes most of the way up the blade, you'll just have to fill back in." That at least should get through to them.

Eric gave him a hard look, then stuck his spade in to show he understood and started gently lifting out little scoopfuls of dirt. David handed Jake back his hoe. He wondered why these three had bothered to sign up, since they clearly didn't want to do any actual work.

He nodded around at them. "Once you've finished here, take a short break. Get some water and shade before you move on." He had to make sure they all stayed sufficiently hydrated.

David turned and resumed his journey toward base camp, casting a final eye over his crew's efforts. At least two new holes should be ready by the time he'd returned. He'd pick up a couple of the motion detectors to bring back, along with a new spade for Greg, and then he could check on the others' progress. Then he would plant the sensors. And if he ended up spending some extra time adjusting the work that had already been done, it would be preferable to having his crew redo it. Particularly when he was this tired.

He wiped the sweat off his brow with his sleeve and drained the last of his water as he passed the markers. He slid the bottle back into the holster at his belt, and his fingers brushed the towel hanging there—that he could have used instead of his sleeve. Maybe *he* needed to spend a few minutes out of the sun.

David sighed as he sat down on the back bench of the small cart he'd driven here in the wee hours. Thankfully it had a canopy to provide some shade. He took his time refilling his water bottle as he let his eyes drift around. Sgt. Rossiter had disappeared once more, and the guards remained as immobile as they'd ever been. David wondered if their attitude had anything to do with the complicated schedule.

His crew was the only one working outside the perimeter wall. In addition to the protection detail, a system had been set up for when and how to open what gates, depending on which section of the buffer zone they were working on a given day. One of the large carts picked up the students and brought them out in the morning and came to take them back in the afternoon. That alone would've been simple.

David wanted to arrive much earlier than his crew, though, and leave later. Ken needed to have access anytime to check on things, and Jeffrey didn't know from day to day when he could come to do his part. And which gate would be most convenient for everybody to use would keep changing, too.

Still, everyone needed to do their part, and the guards were falling down on the job, or would be if the wall wasn't propping them up. David sighed and let his head lean back as he set aside his gripes.

After a moment his head snapped up. He could not continue like that or he'd end up more confused and disoriented than he was already becoming. He forced himself to keep drinking more water and just sitting there in the shade. He tried to sit up straighter and focus his thoughts on the supplies he'd need to gather and what he'd do once he returned to the work area. It would be more peaceful once the cart had come and taken his crew away. Maybe he could cheat and get some of their work done.

"David!" Eric's voice.

Standing up off the back of the buggy and turning that way, David saw Eric and his two hangers-on arriving for their rest break. He must've been wool-gathering far longer than he'd realized. Or Eric and his friends hadn't done the job.

"David!"

Eric had his hoe propped on his shoulder, then started swinging it about aimlessly, and the others followed suit. David stared at them. He wondered if they had any idea just how dangerous that kind of tom-foolery could be. He headed in their direction to give them warning.

Eric stopped, swinging the point of his hoe down to the ground as David approached. Stan stepped forward, resting his spade over his shoulder again. "Look here—it's not right that a freshman like you gets to be in charge. Ordering us seniors around."

"You're juniors, not seniors. FedU's only been going for three years. There are no seniors." David was beginning to think that a pack of wolves might be the more apt analogy. There were wolves on the mountains.

"Pedantic snot. We're *your* seniors."

David stood firm. "Regardless, I've been placed in charge. If you have a problem with that, I suggest you take it up with *my* boss."

Stan started what looked to be a snide reply, but Eric waved him back down. "Listen, we can make an arrangement just between us. Let your boss believe you're running things if you want. But we should be giving the orders."

David started shaking his head while Eric was still speaking. That way would be a complete disaster. "You don't yet know the job, what you're doing. And this is important work."

Eric stretched his lips thin. "Oh, I think we've got the hang of things now."

David stood there, staring at the three of them for a while, wondering if they could really be serious about such nonsense. Then he heard the whine of a cart approaching. Eric and his cohorts glanced over David's shoulder, then started toward the water keg.

Turning around, David saw Ken driving a buggy into the base camp, with an unfamiliar officer in the seat beside him and Sgt. Rossiter hanging onto the back bench. He sighed. This only postponed a confrontation with Eric and his friends. Though maybe he wouldn't be as tired when that time finally came.

Ken parked the cart, and all three climbed out and headed straight for David. Ken waved his hand around. "David, this is Lt. Henson. Lieutenant, this is one of my best men, David Belue. He's one of the FURC students and he's supervising here."

David nodded at Ken. "Boss." He ignored Rossiter but nodded at Henson, who looked intelligent, and sharp in his uniform. "Lieutenant."

Ken continued the introduction. "Lt. Henson is Colonel Gray's representative. He's been charged with overseeing the defenses." While Gray sat in his air-conditioned office twiddling his thumbs was the implication. David was familiar with Ken's opinion of the man.

He thought the lieutenant seemed nice enough, though, even offering to shake hands, which David accepted.

"Good to meet you, Mr. Belue." Henson spoke with a slight British accent and a twinkle in his eye. Then the man turned back to Ken. "I need to have a word with Sgt. Rossiter." He waved to the sergeant and strolled off toward the security fence. Rossiter followed. David wondered how much the lieutenant knew about the situation out here.

"How are things going?" Ken asked.

David was tempted to keep his problems to himself, offer some vague assurances—but he needed to be forthright with his boss. "It's much slower going than I'd hoped. The recruits are taking their sweet time and still having trouble with the work, and I don't know how to motivate them."

Ken scratched his bare upper lip. "I'm confident you can manage."

"Why don't you just put Jeffrey in charge? Let me get back in the trenches and do what I do best." *And maybe this vital work that so urgently needs doing will be done in time.*

There was a hard glint in Ken's eye as he looked at David. "This is where I want you. You know the work, and you know how to get it done right. Show these recruits." His boss cleared his throat and continued, "Your promotion's not a test, you know. It's not a temporary trial to see if you can measure up. I know you can. So stick with it."

David felt his heart sink into his stomach as his mind filled with images of doing this job for the rest of his life. It was *always* supposed to be temporary, part-time. Bad enough the crisis had turned it full-time, now the situation had somehow made the job permanent. He liked and respected his boss, but he didn't want to *become* Ken.

He looked at the man he admired and found he couldn't bring himself to say any of that—not here and now. "What if I mess everything up?"

Ken grunted. "You know what I always say, or you should by now. Do what's right, do your best—"

"And blank the consequences."

Ken smiled wide. "Keep at this job long enough and you'll start swearing proper."

David glanced at his watch. "The big cart will be here soon to pick up the crew, and they'll be done for the day. Jeffrey and I may work a bit longer."

Ken nodded and turned to Lt. Henson who had come back without the sergeant, then looked back at David. "Well, let me know if you need anything."

The lieutenant glanced at David, and then started scratching his nose. "Why don't you go on ahead, Mr. Cameron? I'm not quite finished here."

David's boss shrugged and climbed in the cart. David and the lieutenant watched Ken turn the cart around and trundle off all on his own.

Lt. Henson caught David's eye and gestured out toward the security fence on the far side of the base camp. There stood one of the men who'd supposedly been guarding the crew, scanning the forest beyond with his rifle held firmly in his hands.

"I had a strong word with Sgt. Rossiter—about keeping your men safe. He should be taking care of the other guard right now."

David sighed. The day was already almost over, and there would probably be new guards tomorrow. Hopefully Rossiter would make sure they did their jobs, too, but he'd probably think David had gone over his head. The sergeant looked the type to cause trouble over something like that.

Still, David was grateful to Henson and wanted him to know. "Thank you for taking care of that."

Henson shrugged. "Sometimes you have to take a hard line, but you don't earn your men's respect by letting them walk all over you. So I chewed out the sergeant. Rossiter is responsible for those men, and I reminded him of the fact."

If only it were that easy. "I wish I could have the same effect on my crew." David tried to smile. "But they won't take the situation seriously, and the work is going far too slow. How long will it take to finish preparations? If an attack does come, it could come at any time, and we're nowhere near ready."

The lieutenant shook his head. "I wouldn't worry about that, if I were you."

"Don't worry?"

"These preparations would all be well and good if you were expecting to have to repel a biker gang, or a horde of ravenous zombies." Henson chuckled to himself.

David found himself glaring at his new friend. "It's not really a subject for levity."

"No, it's no joke. I served with the British military for a few years. Their government actually had plans for both. Soccer hooligans rather than bikers, but we'd be better off dealing with the biker gangs."

"But what kind of attack *might* we have to deal with then?" No one had yet said. Not it any detail.

"*If* an attack comes, it'll likely be an assault by the National Guard. A full-on military strike. These are highly trained soldiers with a complete arsenal. You know the governor's been using them to impose martial law, but what you'll have seen doesn't begin to show what they're capable of."

David must have let himself get dehydrated. He felt dizzy and was having a hard time taking in what the lieutenant was saying. "Even more reason to try and get the defenses up as fast as possible."

But Henson was shaking his head. "If it comes down to a fight, we're not going to stand much of a chance anyway. Best hope for a political solution." The man smiled kindly at David. "That's no excuse not to do the best you can, though."

The lieutenant nodded and walked off. Headed to find Ken, probably, but David wasn't paying any attention. David was considering the circumstances surrounding them, the dire situation they faced and the role he was playing. It was impossible. But he'd do what was right, which was the best job he could.

There was something much more important he needed to be doing, though. He needed to pray.

Chapter 4

A Hard Day's Night

5:45 p.m. Thursday, November 28th

KAT bounded down the wide marble stairs, almost charging right into the middle of a brawl. She'd just changed for work and was tempted to skirt around them and hurry on so she wouldn't be late, but she couldn't do that. She had a responsibility—as a security officer, and she was wearing her cap, and also as the daughter of the director. She had a duty that superseded the clock.

She considered the two combatants, neither of whom she recognized. The blond Nordic guy was taller and broader, but the short brown-haired kid looked scrappy. Both had athletic builds, but they weren't really going after each other. Yet. They just glared and shoved each other roughly, swinging the occasional fist in a way that probably passed for a friendly pat among these macho types.

Still, unless Kat intervened the hostilities would likely escalate. A ragged ring of student onlookers had already formed around the edges to enjoy the show, and she scanned the crowd for possible assistance. She couldn't find any, though she believed she'd discovered the cause of the confrontation. She tried to think of some way to diffuse the situation. She knew that the last thing she should do was step into the middle of that fight.

She stepped in between the two men, shoving a palm in each of their faces and pushing them back. "Now. If you two—"

Screaming pain.

Kat's head was yanked back, and tears flooded her eyes. It felt like her hair was being torn from its roots, and it took her a second to realize that was exactly what was happening.

The moment she understood, Kat began back-pedalling into the girl behind her, easing the pull on her scalp, and kept driving backward until she ran her assailant into the wall behind them. A sharp elbow to the woman's midriff got Kat's hair out of the woman's fist, and pitched her attacker's face forward over Kat's shoulder. Kat reached back for a handful of hair herself and pulled as she dropped, lifting with her hip to throw the woman over and onto the floor in front of her.

The woman's arms flailed wildly, claws searching for Kat's face. Kat snatched one flying wrist and used it to twist the woman over onto her front, pushing the air and the fight out of her. She pulled a zip-tie out of her pocket and bound the woman's hands. Then she checked for pulse and respiration. The girl seemed disoriented, her breath was rapid and ragged, but the pulse was strong and steady.

Kat rose to her feet and looked over to where the two idiots had stopped their altercation and stood staring at her, their mouths gaping open like landed trout. She took a couple steps toward the miserable creatures before she noticed her crumpled cap lying on the ground. She sighed and picked it up.

Ignoring her still smarting scalp, she focused on the two boys who were now trying to look like sheep. "Bloody morons." Which wasn't profanity, as she had noticed they did have some cuts and scrapes. And were clearly lacking in intelligence.

The girl who had seemingly sparked all this did start using some profanity. She must have become aware of her situation—or at least that trussed up on the floor as she was, she no longer looked like a prize to be fought over.

Kat glanced at the woman briefly before returning her attention to the would-be gladiators. "You two. Go, now. Get yourselves over to the clinic and seen to." They started off, but Kat called them back. "As soon as the sisters let you go, try and do something useful with yourselves."

The tall blond whined. "We've already finished work for the day."

"What do you do? Who's your supervisor?"

"We're building the perimeter defense. You're not going report us, are you?"

"Of course I'm going to file a report. But there are different ways to write this up. If you do what I told you to do, then maybe you won't end up working for the janitorial staff."

They took this for a final dismissal and trotted away. Kat frowned. She wondered if she'd let them off too easy, but only time would tell. She felt sure they weren't being worked hard enough, though, if they still had energy at the end of the day to engage in this kind of buffoonery. Kat, certainly, should not have to be dealing with them.

And she shouldn't be getting her hair pulled by some troublemaking tart, either. She'd heard the stories, but such a thing had never happened to her before. She needed to make sure it never happened again.

Kat went over to her catch and lifted the girl to her feet by the armpits. The subdued woman stuck to a sullen glare while she was being herded out of the building into the gathering dusk. Kat prodded her along as fast as she could without causing her to stumble and fall.

Thankfully, Security HQ was fairly close to the student dormitories—probably by design. She still ended up arriving a few minutes late. Pushing her charge ahead of her into the lobby, she found Lisa leaning on the duty desk, waiting.

Kat deposited her baggage on a far seat before crossing over to offer her colleague a weak grin. "I really did try to get here on time." She felt the need to offer up some kind of an excuse. "Circumstances intervened." She liked Lisa, the only other female officer, and she didn't want their budding friendship to stall over this.

Lisa smiled. It was weak and tired, but it was a genuine smile. "The first time you're late, and only by a few minutes, and you're already apologizing." She swung the gate open for Kat. "I'm just glad you volunteered to extend your hours so I don't have to work a full double."

Kat glanced back at her prisoner, slumped forward in a hard plastic chair in the lobby. Lisa just shook her head. "Leave her. We'll move her to the conference room before I go off shift, put her in with the others."

Kat followed Lisa to the break room where they both sat and rested for a few moments. She thought about Lisa's page-boy cut. It certainly looked good on Lisa, with her dirty blonde hair, and it was short.

Finally Kat had to ask. The whole point of shift change, after all, was to catch up on everything that was happening. "So, who's in the conference room and why are we putting that creature in there with them?"

Lisa frowned. "It's full of similar bad actors, so she'll fit right in. Most of them we wouldn't be turning over to the local sheriff, even if we could, which we obviously can't now—" She paused for breath, "and we don't have the facilities to hold them here, so we're just keeping them comfortable until someone from Admin can find the time to come over and give them a stern talking to."

Kat grinned despite what she was hearing. She loved talking to Lisa since she barely had to utter a single word herself. "A stern talking to? Please tell me that's someone's idea of a joke."

"It's a poor one if it is. They're supposed to be sending the deputy director herself at least. That one's not going to be all warm and fuzzy with these folk, you can tell just by looking at her." Kat herself wished Ms. Belue were more charismatic, actually—perhaps then she would do a better job of defending the administration.

Anyway, she had relaxed enough to enjoy a cup of coffee. She got up and grabbed the pot and ges-

Chapter 4

tured with it to Lisa who shook her head. Kat asked, "What about—where's Chief Nelson?" She'd almost said Tony, which wouldn't have been professional, and she was determined to be professional.

"As usual our boss is out and about somewhere tending to business, or so he says. It may be one of his girlfriends. I'm convinced he's wooing them on the clock, since he doesn't have the spare time anymore. So he'd about have to be, wouldn't he?"

Kat sighed and sat down to sip her coffee. Lisa was one of those convinced that Tony was secretly a Latin lothario. Kat knew better, but she also knew the futility of saying so. "Other than a roomful of ruffians, all's quiet on the battlefield?"

Lisa nodded and grabbed her purse as she stood. "Kat, you and I've been getting along okay, haven't we? So please don't take offense. But whose side is you mother on anyway?"

Kat took a big gulp of her rapidly cooling coffee before answering. She was surprised that Lisa knew Caroline was her mother—it wasn't exactly a secret, but most people didn't seem to be aware of the fact. Lots of people did know her as the daughter of the director though, which was bad enough.

She *wasn't* surprised by Lisa's opinion of Caroline, though. "I know she sounds like she's always attacking us—" Her mother did bend over backward to make sure critics of the administration got their points made and then some, "but she's just trying to do her job."

Trying to help in her own inimitable way, like making sure everyone knew the supplies of beef and chocolate were running out. They hadn't yet. But it was just a matter of time, and Caroline only made people anxious by always reminding them.

Lisa shook her head, but refrained from adding anything more. "I'll help you move that woman, but then I've got to go before I fall on my face."

"No, that's alright, I can handle her. You go on home to your kid." Over fourteen hours on the clock showed—Lisa was starting to run out of words.

Kat got up again and escorted Lisa through the lobby and out the door before turning to address her prisoner. She thought about giving the girl a stern talking to herself. But between late mornings working for her mother and ten-hour shifts for Security, she'd better start conserving her energy for where it would count.

Just as she was hauling the sleepy transgressor to her feet, three of the student recruits shuffled in through the front door. Two were brand new, but thankfully the other was the business-like Susan—probably because she was a business major.

Introductions could wait. "Susan, would you help me escort the prisoner to her luxury accommodations?" Which Susan likely thought to be a joke.

Chapter 4

Susan nodded briskly and came over to take one of the girl's arms. As they dragged the listless form down the hall, Kat belatedly realized that she'd not asked the woman for her name, or for the names of the two boys who'd been fighting over her. Which reminded Kat of something else.

Susan held their charge while Kat unlocked the conference room door and checked inside. Only four miscreants—two boys that must be other students, a sour looking middle-aged woman, and an older man who looked to be sleeping off an early day's drink. Kat added to their number and locked them back in again.

Susan must've been surprised by the situation, but she didn't show it. "Any instructions?"

"Someone from Admin should stop by at some point to take care of them. Supposedly the deputy director." Though Kat wouldn't hold her breath. "Until then, check on them when you can, but only when an officer is here to help. And when you do, I'd appreciate if you could do the intake on the one we just deposited. I'll write the report when I take my break."

Susan nodded.

Kat pulled out her FURCS pad before she forgot, and used her security pass to take a look at the clinic's patient logs. The two boys had followed orders, and now she had their names.

Susan followed Kat back out to the lobby, where the other two volunteers still waited, both in their teal windbreakers and caps. Kat looked them both up and down thoroughly. "Susan, if you wouldn't mind taking the duty desk while I'm out on patrol?"

Susan nodded and sat down in the chair behind the desk and began examining the activity logs.

Kat swung the gate open and walked over to the new recruits. She started with the tall, lanky guy. "Name?"

"Paul, mam."

Kat winced. She might have shared a class with either of these two, though she didn't recall. "I bet you play basketball, Paul."

"No, mam, I'm not much one for sports. I'm a physics major."

Kat turned to the pudgy girl with long brown hair and rosy cheeks. "And you?"

"I'm Hope. I'm studying English Literature, and I enjoy a nice game of badminton." Hope smiled.

Kat nodded. Policy required her to take someone with her on patrol. Either another officer, which was rarely practical, or two of the student recruits, who were all now considered to be officer trainees. She'd take these two. She could get to know them and give them some experience while she was at it.

She shooed them out the door and into the night with a slight sensation of shock. The fading light of dusk had disappeared while she'd been taking care of business.

Which wasn't unusual in itself. But it made Kat wonder if the two jobs and the long hours were taking their toll. She'd even forgotten to ask Lisa where the woman had her hair done. She definitely needed to find a way to get out of working for her mother.

She shook her head and stalked off toward the Green, expecting the newbies to catch up—and they did, with a lot of huffing and puffing and swinging of their arms as they walked.

"Why aren't we taking a cart?" Hope puffed.

"Because." Kat walked along, scanning everywhere as she talked over her shoulder. "Sometimes it's better to use your own two feet."

"Why do we patrol anyway? People can call for help on their FURCS pads if they need to, right?"

"Not always, no." Kat slowed her pace as they approached the Green. "And it's important people see us—understand that we're around, somewhere." Even moving slow, she'd give both of them plenty of exercise.

They turned onto the wide sidewalk circling the turf, where the lights designed to look like Victorian gas lamps provided enough illumination to discourage trouble. But the romantic atmosphere helped picnicking couples enjoy their evening. Which they still managed to do, despite everything.

Kat paid no particular attention to anything or anyone—she simply let her subconscious take note and trusted her intuition to raise a red flag. If there *were* anything she needed to notice—although this area did need to be patrolled, the need was greater elsewhere. But first, she'd have to break the two newbies in.

Halfway around the Green, Hope ventured another question. "Don't you need a gun?"

Kat grinned to herself. "I do *have* a gun. Every officer is assigned a firearm. But they're kept locked up safe in a small armory back at headquarters unless they're needed." She glanced over at Paul and then back at Hope to see if they were both listening. "Residents aren't allowed to bring any weapons into the compound, so it might be provocative if *we* carried guns around." And people had always behaved themselves, for the most part.

By the time they'd done the full circuit, Kat was itching to check out some of the more out of the way locations. The places the tram didn't travel. Where people alone in the dark might find trouble—those who were looking for it and those who weren't.

They swept past the student dorms and turned toward headquarters. Kat gently rubbed her wrist and checked the time. Even with the slow pace, they hadn't been out a full hour yet. Her trainees were probably ready for a break by now, but the patrol would continue. She did think they'd had enough exercise, though.

Kat smiled at the weary and winded pair. "Are you ready for a break? How about we take out one the carts?" That got Hope beaming.

Kat led them around the side to where the buggies were parked. "Who wants to drive this thing?" She took a key from her pocket and held it up.

Paul nodded, "I think I can manage it." He took the key and slid into the driver's seat of the nearest cart. Kat took the seat next to him. Hope plopped onto the back bench with a sigh.

Kat pointed Paul in the direction she wanted to go, and they headed out again. "Paul, how much of the layout of this place are you familiar with?"

For some reason the man blushed. "Only where I need to go, as it were. Should I have been studying a map or something?"

"You can learn the lay of the land as you go, but it wouldn't hurt to study a map—and to carry it with you, at least while you're on duty."

Kat pointed again. "Take that path. It goes between the two research wings and swings round to the east side of the Ag Center."

As they traveled on, they entered quieter, less populated areas. They continued for half an hour, circling the Agriculture Center, then heading back toward the worker dormitories, where they'd start encountering more people. The path began to curve down a gentle slope, and a group of men appeared ahead of them. The one in front stopped and held his arms out to bar their way.

Kat reached over and put her hand on Paul's shoulder. "Stop." Paul eased the cart to a halt and looked to her for more. Kat made out four of them, not quite steady on their feet, and she wished they were falling down drunk instead.

The man in front had a mass of curly black hair and a prominent nose. "Hey! Who do you think you are? Riding around like royalty while we—" And then he burped.

Hope, leaning forward from the back of the buggy to watch, giggled.

As Kat climbed out of the cart she talked to Paul and Hope in a low, clear voice. "You two stay here. If there's any trouble, take off right away. I'll call for help if I need it."

Paul objected, "We're supposed to stay with you. If you think you may need help—"

"You're first duty is to protect yourselves and each other. If you can stay close enough to keep an eye on things, fine, but first get far enough away to be safe."

Kat leaned in for a final word. "Once you're out of danger, you can call headquarters and tell them to send help, and let them know where we are. And if you fail to get through on your FURCS pads, it never hurts to scream for help."

Kat moved away from the cart and walked on to where she stood a few feet in front of the four men. "Are you going to let us pass?"

"Well, let me think about that, honey." Big nose looked over her shoulder and gestured to one of the other men, who started circling around Kat, toward Paul and Hope.

Kat turned her head enough to follow that man, and to see the cart in the corner of her eye. She was pleased to see Paul follow her orders and take off in a wide arc away from the fellow, then start speeding back up the slope. So some physics majors *could* be smart. But now one of the men was behind Kat.

Big Nose laughed loud. "Looks like your friends have abandoned you."

She ignored him. At least they weren't rushing her. They probably lacked the intelligence to coordinate their tactics. She'd an additional advantage that she was sober, and another in their clear belief they had *her* at a disadvantage. She'd allow them to think they were in control.

Their leader suddenly let his arms drop. "Hey! I know who you are." That wasn't good. "You're *his* daughter." He turned back to his friends. "This is the director's brat. Her dad got us into this mess." And the looks on their faces got uglier.

For perhaps the first time, Kat wished she were known as her mother's daughter, but she didn't like hearing them bad mouth her dad. *At least Paul and Hope should be safe now.*

She saw no more point in delaying, then. Time to force them to make a move, and Kat immediately knew what move she wanted them to make.

Kat put her arms up in front of her. "Please, I don't want any trouble." Though clearly *they* did. She backed up a step toward the man that had circled around behind her. She would give them what they were expecting.

Big Nose advanced toward her, and she kept a close watch on his face, saw him start to grin. She could feel the other one behind her—not too close, but they clearly felt they had her trapped now.

Kat stepped back again, pulling the leader in. Like reeling in a fish. Her senses were finely attuned to every detail, and her timing had to be perfect. She moved back just a little too slow as he strode toward her. And created just the moment she wanted.

Big Nose lunged forward, swinging his right fist. Kat half-stepped forward at an angle, pivoted inside his center of gravity like a spinning top, and heard him crashing into his friend behind her. While she darted ahead.

The other two had a moment of confusion, probably exacerbated by their inebriation. She'd already reached one of them when he belatedly made a grab for her, but she was already behind him, kicking him through the back of his knee and pushing him to the ground. The other one was still standing and staring at her as she pulled out a pair of zip-ties and started binding the hands of the guy down on the ground.

She glanced over and gave him his instructions. "Just lie face down on the ground and put your arms behind your back."

As she moved over to zip-tie that one, she noticed that the first two had now started to untangle themselves from each other.

By the time Tony and Officer Kirkland arrived, speeding down the slope in one of the big carts, Kat had gotten all four lined up sitting on one side of the path with their arms bound behind them and hanging their heads. In shame, she hoped.

Tony pulled the cart up beside her, and Kat saw both men were grinning. Still coming down the hill were Paul and Hope in the other buggy.

"Need a ride, Kat?"

She looked at the miserable quartet and shook her head. "You can give these guys a ride, though. To you know where. I'll just take Paul and Hope and finish my patrol."

She left the two men still grinning.

Chapter 5
Not Being Paranoid

10:55 a.m. Saturday, November 30th

DAVID examined Eric's work, nodding as he hand-ed the man a yellow flag. Good enough, and he'd fix it later. "Plant that next to the hole. Jeffrey and I will take care of the rest."

He didn't need to suggest a break, because Eric took one after each hole he finished regardless. He remained surly, but at least the man didn't actively cause trouble anymore.

Indeed, Eric seemed strangely subdued lately. He and his friends still refused to take the job seri-ously, but the rest had improved dramatically, and the crew was starting to make some real progress. Maybe the reality of the situation was setting in.

David turned to see what needed his attention next and felt a flash of irritation when he spied Sgt. Rossiter over by the base camp—again wandering around and fiddling with his pad. The sergeant did little else when he was here, which was less and less all the time. Still, Rossiter had spoken to each guard rotation until they all knew they couldn't slack off.

But David had been mulling over Rossiter's behavior ever since yesterday morning's conversation with Ken. Thursday afternoon, David's crew had finally finished the first section he'd marked off. So yesterday before dawn, he'd gone out to mark off a new work area, and had then begun moving the base camp to a new location—by himself until his boss had shown up to give him a hand.

David had asked him again about Fiona and the girls, sure that Ken must miss them since all outside communication had been cut off. The man couldn't even talk with them. Ken had simply shrugged and said his family was likely safer there than they'd be here. Then he'd made the gruff comment that had taken root in David's mind. That if he really needed to talk to his family, he'd try to find a spot near the perimeter where he could get a signal through to an outside cell tower with his regular phone.

Which had started David wondering if that was what Sgt. Rossiter was always doing when he wandered around the buffer zone. David hadn't seen if the sergeant was fiddling with his FURCS pad or a normal cell phone. Nor did he have any idea whether the man had a family on the outside or not, or at all—hadn't even paid enough attention to recall if Rossiter wore a ring.

He noticed the sergeant tuck away whatever the device was and stalk off. Another of the man's frequent disappearing acts, it thwarted David's notion of trying to get a closer look to see if it was a FURCS pad or a regular cell. He looked around at his crew, but saw nothing needing his urgent attention.

So he walked over to the base camp, where Jeffrey was eating his lunch before he began going over the ground they'd finished so far. David wiped his brow with his towel as he approached.

"Jeff." He waited until the man looked up. "I want to take my lunch break inside. If you wouldn't mind keeping an eye on the crew 'til I get back?"

Jeff pushed his glasses back up his nose and smiled. "No problem. I can watch them while I finish eating."

"It might be a long break."

Jeffrey only nodded and went back to his lunch. David didn't waste any more time. He strode off in the same direction Rossiter had gone, little doubt in his mind where the man was headed. He just needed to catch up to him before the sergeant got lost on the inside.

David caught sight of the man soon enough and slackened his pace, because he didn't want to draw the man's attention. He wondered why he felt the need to go to such lengths to exercise his curiosity. He'd likely find a simple explanation for the man's absences, and if Rossiter were trying to call someone on the outside, it probably *was* his family.

Still, the sergeant *could* be trying to contact the governor's people. Maybe David was simply being paranoid, but he couldn't help but speculate about the less pleasant possibilities. He'd feel better once he'd satisfied himself in his own mind.

He followed Rossiter to the north gate, usually called the Ag Center gate, the one currently being used by David's crew and anyone else needing to go back and forth from the buffer zone. There was a matching gate in the fence here. Workers used to go out to tend the apiary and the livestock herds and some experimental fields—all of which lay outside the compound and who knew what would happen to those now. Because a week ago the fence had been sealed. No one had gone out since.

None of the other three gates in the perimeter wall were being used right now, so naturally the Ag Gate would be the way both the sergeant and David would re-enter the compound. This was nothing unusual. Still, David followed the man through the gate and back inside.

David tried to keep a discreet distance as the sergeant weaved his way around to the front of the Ag Center and stopped at the tram station. David understood that here he'd only one choice. So he strolled up and sat down on the bench at the far end and tried to appear as if he were minding his own business. He couldn't keep a close eye on the sergeant without looking conspicuous. It would lend some credence to his suspicions, though, if Rossiter were to abandon the tram station now.

David tried to be casual. He checked his watch against the posted schedule, even though he knew it was outdated. He was attempting to keep his mind away from dwelling on the fact that he was trailing someone. So he focused his thoughts on lunch. He was just another worker on his lunch break, going somewhere to eat. Which reminded him of the dinner last night at his mom's house.

He'd left work at the same time as his crew, so he'd have time to swing by his dorm room and pick up a few things. Becoming more and more uncomfortable living right down the hall from the recruits he supervised, he'd decided to stay at his mother's house. He'd thought it would be easier. He'd stayed there overnight on occasion, when it was closer to where he needed to be in the morning.

Now it would make for a longer trek to work. That had still seemed preferable, though, and he'd arrived at what was essentially his own home only to have the door opened by Crystal, the blonde Scandinavian student worker who kept house for his mom. Crystal was a junior and very mature, and beautiful, but still a fellow student. David couldn't think of her as a housekeeper, especially not when she often wore tight sweaters and tighter jeans.

The screech of the arriving tram jolted David out of his reverie. He forced his mind away from Crystal the same way he'd had to the previous evening. He barely prevented himself from checking to see if the sergeant was still there—instead, he took his time standing and ambled his way over to the tram. He was rewarded to see the sergeant jumping onboard. He walked to the next car down, climbed on, and sighed as he sat on the thinly padded vinyl. Now all he had to do was stay alert and watch.

He stared straight ahead while the tram glided along, trying to think of lunch. He had too much on his mind to be particularly hungry, but he knew he'd have to eat something somewhere if he didn't want to be fainting on the job after he got back.

The pasta last night had been delicious, but that would be too far to travel, even if Crystal were there to cook for him. Which she wouldn't be.

Crystal wasn't needed full-time at his mother's house, so she had taken a second part-time position, which she left for late in the morning and then returned from late in the afternoon. Though there was no apparent need, she'd managed to prevail upon David's mother to live in their home now. He'd only found that out after he'd announced his own intention to move back in.

He wrenched his thoughts away from that awkward subject and tried to see how far the tram had traveled so far. He risked a casual glance around. Rossiter remained onboard, and they were just coming up to the Community Hall station. The sergeant stayed onboard as the tram pulled away.

David managed to stay alert and keep his mind from wandering again for another ten minutes or so as they traveled through the residential area where he and his mother and Crystal now lived in the same house. The tram stopped just before the main thoroughfare. Rossiter jumped off, and David realized where the man must be headed.

He had often walked down here in the mornings to meet Ken not far from this very same tram stop, across from the Guard Headquarters. He sighed as he slid off his seat and onto the sidewalk. A simple explanation after all.

He strolled toward the building thinking fast. He surely couldn't just walk into the place without a good reason. He needed an explanation that would hold up, even if they turned him away, so it would be best to tell the truth. Or what he could of the truth.

David found a guard with a clipboard waiting in the lobby and walked straight up to the man, asking his own question before he was addressed. "Is Sgt. Rossiter here?"

The guard looked David up and down thoroughly. "And you are?"

"David Belue. I head the work crew out beyond the perimeter wall, and the sergeant is in charge of the guard detail assigned to us."

The guard nodded to himself. "The sergeant got in only a couple minutes ago, but he's in with Colonel Gray. He can't be disturbed." The man frowned at David. "He could be a long time. You *could* wait here—or you could just go back to work and talk to the sergeant when he returns."

David paused as if he were considering his options. "If Sgt. Rossiter actually stayed around for a while, I wouldn't have had to come looking for him." It seemed the sergeant had come here on legitimate business—now David needed to make sure his own actions appeared justified. "He's always taking off for hours at a time."

The guard looked annoyed. "Does your detail stay?" He didn't even wait for David's nod. "Then what are you complaining about? Sgt. Rossiter has other duties, so cut the man some slack."

David tried to look penitent, which wasn't hard because he was truly sorry. Now he had his reasonable explanation for the sergeant's absences and felt the fool. Satisfied in his own mind, he'd best leave now—and start thinking again about what to do for lunch. He'd turned to go when he heard his name called.

"Mr. Belue."

David turned to see Lt. Henson coming down the hallway. The guard also turned and saluted.

"He came to see Sgt. Rossiter, sir." He looked as if he wanted to say more, but whatever it was on the tip of the man's tongue, he refrained.

The lieutenant smiled at David. "And of course Rossiter's too busy right now. Since you've come all this way, though, why not let me stand you lunch? Unless you've already eaten?"

David shook his head and stifled a sigh of relief. Another problem solved. Even if the food wasn't any good, he could then head back to work with all this behind him. "It'd be an honor, Lieutenant."

Henson turned to head back down the hall and David followed. He thought it best to continue with his previous explanation. "I feel silly. I never considered that Sgt. Rossiter might have other duties to keep him busy. I was just getting fed up with him hardly ever sticking around."

Henson grinned. "Oh, Colonel Gray uses the sergeant as a general dogsbody. He has the man running errands half the day."

They came to a pair of wide double doors standing open, and Lt. Henson motioned David to enter. "Welcome to the Officers' Mess." He caught David's look. "Just a cafeteria, but we're all ex-military, so we call it what we want."

David nodded. "Is that why you and Ken both call him 'Colonel', while my mom calls him 'Chief'?"

Henson went to stand at the back of the line. "Chief of External Security is his technical rank, but he was a colonel with the Army National Guard. So all of us veterans give him his military rank."

David followed along behind, grabbing a plastic tray and a large bowl of stew. Beef and vegetables. "I see we haven't quite run out of supplies yet."

Henson took a basket of bread to add to his tray and nodded. "There's not much of the fresh stuff left. But I understand there are enough frozen and canned stores to last through half the winter."

Half the winter? That didn't sound good. David moved a basket of the fresh baked rolls onto his own tray and continued down the line. "Gray was in the National Guard? Not Florida's?"

Henson nodded while he used his FURCS pad to pay for their meals. "Yes, as it happens."

"Then the colonel probably knows a lot about how they might attack us." David paused while the lieutenant looked around for a table. "If Governor Roberts retains control of the Guard and does try to attack the compound." David followed Henson to a table in the corner, away from the general hubbub.

After they sat, the lieutenant waited a moment before answering. "I suppose he could be helpful. If he wanted."

David stopped the spoonful of stew headed toward his mouth for a moment, then tried to digest the stew and Henson's words at the same time. His suspicions were returning.

But the lieutenant had already moved on. "You ever consider transferring here? You'd make a good guard. There'd be a lot of tough training, though."

David shook his head. "I'd heard they wanted to start training more guards to defend the compound. Ken even took me to the firing range the other evening to show me how to a handle a gun safely. Tried to teach me how to shoot and hit the target." David raised one side of his mouth between bites. "I think a couple of times I actually managed to hit the white part—out on the edge of the paper."

"Well, it takes lots and lots of practice. You can't expect to start off as a marksman."

"I hardly have the time, and if I did I'd be trying to get in as much of my classes as I could. Most of the other students seem to be finding more time for their studies." *And how much do they work?*

Lt. Henson left the subject there and focused on his food, but David had more serious matters pressing upon his mind. He tried to order his thoughts while he ate.

Gray had been a colonel in the Florida National Guard, which had to be considered the enemy at the moment. According to the lieutenant though, the colonel wasn't being helpful. David knew that from the beginning Gray had left taking care of the compound defense to Henson without seeming to lift a finger himself.

That could be incompetence, or just plain laziness. Surely the director and everyone in authority must know about Gray's history. They'd certainly understand if there were a problem with the colonel, and they'd have done something about it. But they might not know about Sgt. Rossiter.

Know what? That the sergeant spent a lot of his time fiddling with his device out in the buffer zone, or running errands for Chief Gray, didn't amount to actual evidence of anything.

David could tell his mother what he'd seen and heard, but it would be better if he'd something more concrete. Maybe he could pursue that now. After he finished chewing a hunk of bread, he described Rossiter's behavior to the lieutenant.

"Ken said you might be able to find a spot where you could connect to an outside cell tower. My mom said it's unlikely, though, because the fence's electrical field interferes with reception."

David remembered the conversation last night over supper. Everyone knew communication with the outside had been shut down—the FURCSnet restricted phone, internet and satellite. Few people knew that only the director and David's mother had the access codes to alter those restrictions. He had asked his mom if she couldn't make an exception for Ken to call and check on his wife and kids, and she'd refused to even consider it.

"Though she admitted that theoretically someone might be able to find a spot where a call could get through. I thought Rossiter might be trying just that. Of course, he might want to talk with his family. That would be understandable."

At least Henson had listened to David without laughing, or looking at him like he was a fool. He waited a long moment before he responded. "Sgt. Rossiter doesn't have any family to speak of. I think you'd have to be pretty desperate, to go to all that trouble trying to contact someone, but I don't know of anyone who'd mean that much to the sergeant." The lieutenant looked at David. "You're thinking it's possible Rossiter's trying to contact the governor's people on the outside? He could be trying to get a message out to them, I suppose."

"Maybe there's a way we can find out."

Henson shook his head. "I don't know how. The question I have in mind is this—if Rossiter *is* trying to do something, is he acting on his own? Or is it on someone else's behalf?"

David nodded and lowered his voice. "You're talking about Chief Gray."

"The sergeant is a soldier, after all, and used to taking orders. Even if he is doing something untoward, which there's no evidence of, he could be just following instructions." Henson frowned. "I know you don't like Rossiter, but does he strike you as an independent operator?"

David shook his head. "All these errands Gray has the sergeant running. They might be anything." And the potential implications were frightening.

"It's only speculation. There's not the slightest bit of evidence to support any of this." The lieutenant heaved a sigh. "And if Gray were colluding with the enemy, we'd be in real serious trouble. He has command of the entire defense. If he chose to use it. So let's hope this is all in your imagination."

David admitted that he was prejudiced against the sergeant, so it would be best not to jump to any conclusions when there was no evidence. He considered what Henson had just said, though. Colonel Gray could order the guards to open the gates and the fence, and they'd probably just stand by while the tanks rolled in.

David sighed. "Let's hope. We'd be up a creek without a paddle, as we used to say back home."

The lieutenant's smile was grim as he responded, "And it's already pouring down rain." Henson shook his head and looked down at the remains of his meal. "Or maybe we're just worrying too much."

It seemed to David that Henson wasn't going to take it any further himself. Though he wondered if the lieutenant would just follow orders, the way he'd said. He thought Henson was one military man who would balk. He hoped so. He himself needed to do more than hope, though.

"Thanks for dinner. It was good." David picked up his tray and started to leave, but before he went he turned back to the lieutenant. "If I can find some evidence, I will."

He could talk to Ken or his mother about his suspicions, and either of them would at least listen to him, the way Henson had. But it was all supposition, and without any evidence neither would likely be able to act. David could not just sit on his hands, though.

He cogitated all the way back to base camp, and he couldn't see any alternative but to investigate on his own. At least until he found something to substantiate his suspicions.

Chapter 6

Bit of a Dust-Up

6:55 p.m. Saturday, December 7th

KAT jogged up the wide steps outside the Community Hall, feeling great back in her old teal uniform. She welcomed the windbreaker on this cold, crisp night, but she held her brand new cap in her hand. To show off her brand new bob.

She'd arrived at the studio early this morning, before her mother, and promised Stacy a favor—in return for cutting her hair to order and not mentioning it to Caroline. She had been delighted when her mother had come in asking who had done her hair and demanding to know why she hadn't let Stacy do it. She imagined the hairdresser got a quiet chuckle out of it as well.

Kat sailed in through one of the open doors and into the lobby. Despite being opened up and having fans circulating the air, the large crowd was making the place feel stuffy. Many mingled in the lobby. She found many more had already crammed themselves into the main hall, generating a lot of body heat while they waited. Here it had become stuffy *and* warm, and would no doubt get a lot worse.

Still, she kept her windbreaker on and donned her cap, with reluctance—though she understood why Tony had wanted a uniformed presence. She even agreed with his reasoning. He hoped to deter things from getting out of hand, and he'd stationed officers all around the hall—but instead of having them in their proper uniforms, he'd ordered them to wear the teal safety aide outfits. He thought that would be less intimidating at what was supposed to be a civil discussion. Kat just hoped that's what it turned out to be.

She looked to the front of the room and saw the long table set up on the speaking platform, and her father and Ms. Belue already in their seats on one end. At the other end, both chairs remained empty, but two people stood behind the chairs in quiet conversation. She recognized the one as the academic dean for the FURC. The other looked vaguely familiar, but she only knew him as a prominent member of the Residents' Council. She couldn't remember his name, but it had been on this morning's alerts notification memo.

Of course, the center seat also sat empty. Caroline was to be the purportedly objective party that moderated this meeting, and she liked to make an entrance. Kat suspected her mother was in a back room waiting for everyone to be waiting on her. She snorted at the thought. Then she remembered her new haircut wasn't the only reason she was feeling light as air.

She spotted Tony leaning against the wall at the back of the room behind the speakers, and she started making her way through the crowd. She circled around the platform to get where she could talk to him. Nothing would look strange about that. And while she'd been assigned to cover the back of the crowd near the entrance, the meeting wasn't even scheduled to start for a couple of minutes, and these things never began on time anyway.

She gestured at the door behind Tony that had been left ajar. "Caroline back there?"

Tony nodded. "If you want a word with her, better make it quick, then get back to your post. Care's in the first room on the right."

Kat smiled as she breezed past him through the doorway, down the short corridor and into the room indicated. Her mother had appropriated it to use as a green room, to prepare herself. Susan stood just inside like a statue. The capable woman had been made a full security officer—this was her first real assignment.

Caroline looked up from her tiny mirror to see Kat entering the room, and complained. "Couldn't you have assigned an officer to me who was more congenial? Or is there such a person in Security?"

Kat grinned. "We should have assigned Hope. The two of you could've had a nice little chat. But she's not an officer, so that wouldn't have been appropriate for someone of your status."

Her mother simply nodded, surely finding that explanation pleasing. "Under the circumstances, I do appreciate the protection. Though your father is the one putting himself at risk."

Kat sighed. She didn't want to come straight out and agree with her mother, though. "I don't understand people. We were already fairly isolated here, but that becomes a little more definite, and people can't wait to start complaining about it. So far, life hasn't really changed all that much, but people are really getting angry." If Caroline understood other people the way she seemed to, maybe she could shed some light on their behavior.

Her mother shook her head. "It's not about the reality in people's lives, it's about perception. Psychology. They start wanting to do things they aren't allowed to do, precisely because they can't."

Kat shook her own head. That made no sense to her, though it clearly made sense to Caroline. She turned to Susan. "Could you give us a minute?"

Susan gave a pointed looked at her watch and slipped out the door. Kat understood that to be a warning about the time and not a message that Susan would return in a prompt minute.

"Mother, I'm going to have work in Security full-time. Things are getting worse out there, and they need me to work more hours. I need to be fresher for the job. So I won't be showing up at the Media Centre next week." *Or ever again.*

Caroline started to splutter. "But, Katherine. We need the time—"

"To bond, I know. We agreed." Kat tried for a rueful frown. "I agree. But we don't really get to be alone, to get to know each other. And you're always so busy. It's just not working out, Mother."

Caroline opened her mouth to object, but Kat put up a hand to stop her.

"What I think, Mother, is that I should move out of the student dorms and into father's house with you. Then we'll have the opportunity for plenty of mother-daughter bonding." Though Kat didn't intend to spend much time at home.

Caroline's mouth inched into a tiny smile. "It *is* a cute outfit, dear."

"It's not what I usually wear, Mother."

"You know I've got a couple more interns now. And that new blonde appreciates appearances more than you." Caroline shook her red curls lightly. "I'll be fine. You go enjoy playing cop."

Kat tried to fight down elation and irritation at the same time. By now she ought to have stopped being surprised by her mother—she *had* gotten to know the woman better. She'd even come up with this strategy herself. Then Tony had agreed that it would work, and he should know.

Kat looked at her watch. "Good luck tonight." She didn't know what else to say. She didn't think 'break a leg' seemed appropriate, even if Caroline considered this evening to be a performance.

She left with a little wave to Susan and returned to the back of the meeting chamber. She winked at Tony to let him know it had went well and headed for the other side of the room, weaving through the newcomers pushing in from the opposite direction until she reached her post.

Kat was excited, and aside from the heat there was a definite feeling of electricity in the air. She'd better be on her toes.

The hands of the big clock hanging on the back wall ticked over to seven. The two community leaders ended their little talk and took their seats, and more people continued to press into the room from the lobby—students and instructors, laborers and bureaucrats, tradesmen and technicians. It was a huge, diverse crowd, packing the space full.

They had expected as much. Two weeks since everyone's lives had been turned upside down—by the governor's surprising actions and then the compound being locked down.

They'd been sealed off from the outside world, and rumors circulated wildly. So far the only official response since the original announcement had been some vague pronouncements that everything necessary was being done. There remained a complete lack of real news.

Kat didn't blame people for being dissatisfied, but they'd all been privileged to participate in this extraordinary project. Especially when most of the communities around the country were struggling so much these days. The residents had seemed to appreciate their circumstances before, and she found it surprising how quickly they were turning bitter upon encountering a little adversity. She felt extremely grateful herself, though she knew she was even more privileged than most.

She stood and watched the crowd shuffle their feet and listened to their murmuring grow steadily louder for another five minutes. Then a quick hush descended. Caroline Sanderson had appeared.

Kat marveled at the effect her mother had, even as it perplexed her. She herself was immune to this charismatic power Caroline exerted, which was another thing for which she was truly grateful.

Kat was also glad she'd worn her boots with the two-inch heels. For all they made her nearly six feet tall, she still had to stretch to see over the crowd. She'd want to watch what was happening herself.

She'd barely seen her father over the last two weeks, and then he hadn't had time to do more than greet her and ask how she was doing. Or maybe he was withholding the news on purpose.

She'd not had much chance to speak with other students, either. Kat had been spending too much time focusing on her work to talk with those she'd considered friends before. As for those she hadn't been friends with—well, most of her personal interaction these days came in her professional capacity and was not conducive to chit-chat. But at least she loved her job.

The crowd had started to buzz softly again as Caroline took her time waltzing across the platform and taking her seat. Then she cleared her throat into the microphone.

"Friends—and I hope I'm right to call you my friends—I'm sure you'll help me to welcome Dean Kittner and Councilman Radley. They've come forward tonight to represent your concerns about the current circumstances." Caroline waited for both of them to nod an acknowledgment before she continued. "Thank you, Alice. Thank you, George." Those two smiled, but they didn't look happy.

Caroline turned to Kat's father and Verity. "I think everyone here is anxious to get some explanations—about what you're doing to address their concerns, and how you plan to resolve this situation." Apparently Caroline didn't think they needed introduction. "So why don't you start by giving them the answers they came for."

Kat's father propped his elbows on the table and clasped his hands together. He leaned forward and scanned the sea of faces, peering through his glasses as if he were examining a peculiar phenomenon. At least that was the impression he gave.

"Many of you won't believe what I'm about to say, but it's the truth. We don't know what's happening outside. The emergency protocols require an absolute communications blackout, and that's what we've put in place. We don't have any information about what's happening—across the state or across the country. What we need to discuss is the situation right here. What this community needs—"

"Of course we don't believe you!"

Kat stood on her toes trying to spot who had shouted in interruption, but there were too many people jostling around.

"What we need is to be able to leave this place."

"I need to let my family know—"

"My wife lives just over in—"

People kept shouting over each other, started pushing against each other, and Kat found herself being shoved further to the back of the room.

Caroline had her gavel in hand and began banging it enthusiastically, though the crowd paid little attention.

Councilman Radley stood abruptly, sending his chair crashing back against the platform and cutting short the commotion. He looked around the crowd with his jaws clenched. "A better question is what gives them the authority to keep us trapped in here? I know many of you, like myself, have business to conduct on the outside. Others have friends and family they're worried about."

He turned to glare at Kat's father. "What's the deal with the complete cut-off? What gives them the right?" Shouts of approval greeted his words and he continued. "Does it even matter if it's the State or the Feds who're running the show here? I think the director overreacted. I have an idea—"

Radley cut off whatever he would have said as her dad rose to his feet. "As I said two weeks ago, this is federal property and Governor Roberts has no authority to appropriate it. We have evidence that he's prepared to try and take over this community by force, and we have no way of knowing what he might plan to do here if he did take control.

"As I also stated in my original announcement, the FURC Charter gives me full authority to initiate the emergency protocols in case of a threat to this community, and requires certain steps be taken. All for the sole purpose of protecting this community. As soon as we're able to do something about communicating with your loved ones, or—"

People in the crowd started shouting again. Caroline whacked her gavel down. Radley growled at Kat's father, but she couldn't hear over the crowd. She saw her dad start shaking his head.

The crowd's shouts merged into a continuous deafening roar and everyone started seething back and forth like violent waves. Kat had to fight to keep her footing. She saw Tony tapping her dad on the shoulder and her mom already standing up. Dean Alice sat frozen in her chair, and Radley shook a fist while his words drowned.

Kat watched in horror as someone pushed the person in front of them so hard they fell to the ground unheeded by the crowd. She started shoving her own way forward to try and reach him. Down on his hands and knees on the floor, that unfortunate could soon be trampled underfoot.

Kat herself was roughly knocked by one person into another like a pinball, but she was able to use that to propel herself further into the crowd. At last she reached the young man, probably a student, who had now curled into a fetal position. A gash on his forehead was bleeding. Kat knelt over him and tried to shield him with her arms while she figured out what to do.

She couldn't lift him while he was rolled up into a ball. And she wasn't sure how she could get him out even if she managed to get him to his feet. All of a sudden, the crowd broke forward. Kat felt a foot slamming into her back, but she rocked with the impact, and then the tide was breaking around them. When it passed, she dared to raise her head for a glimpse.

It took her only a second to assess the situation. Tony must have herded her father and mother and Verity off the platform and into the rooms beyond. That door was closed and presumably locked, because several people were pounding on it with their fists. Radley and Kittner had huddled in the opposite corner, but the crowd was ignoring them for the moment.

Kat tucked her head back down and wrapped herself around her charge. Everything was out of control. She couldn't imagine what would happen next, and she doubted those in the crowd understood what they were doing any better than she. They weren't even people anymore. They had become a single rabid beast, mindless and arbitrary in its violence.

Kat didn't understand how this had happened, how it could have happened. These people *knew* how to behave themselves, even if they *were* frustrated and angry. Her dad hadn't gotten a chance to even address their concerns. They were *that* mad. Then Kat realized what that could mean for her.

If they were that aggrieved with her father, she didn't want to think about what they would do if she were recognized here and now as his daughter. She remembered one particular encounter. She'd handled those guys easily enough, but this situation was already much more perilous.

She wrapped her arms tighter around the boy and tucked in her head. Hopefully the anonymity of the uniform would protect her. The new cap had been lost in all the jostling, but Kat's new hairstyle looked completely different from the old and that should help, too. If these people started thinking clearly enough to see through all that, they'd likely be calming down as well.

But instead of waiting to see when or if that happened, Kat needed to consider an exit strategy. She lifted her head slightly and tried to scan the room through her bangs. The crowd had all surged ahead of her, and with everyone facing the opposite direction, she might be able to slip away unnoticed. She doubted she could drag the injured boy along with her, though—not without attracting attention.

She could not abandon him. There had to be a way to get both herself and the boy to safety. She would have to try talking to him softly, and get him to follow her instructions. She couldn't manage this without his cooperation. Kat found herself wishing she had her mother's ability to charm people.

She felt a presence coming up behind her, saw a mountain of shadow cast around her, and she tried to prepare herself for the worst.

A gruff voice boomed. "What in flaming tarnation is going on here?!"

Kat turned her head to see a figure blocking one of the exits. Contractor Ken Cameron. He strode past her and the boy and stood in front of them as he thundered at the crowd again. "Have you folks lost your blasted minds?"

Kat shifted and looked around the back of the room as several more burly figures entered the hall. Apparently Cameron and his crew had arrived to the meeting late. In this particular instance, late was a vast improvement over never.

Feeling safer with this distraction, Kat slowly shifted to a standing crouch and tried to ease the boy to his feet. When she looked up again, it was obvious—the fever had broken. People were looking around them as if in daze.

Then the door at the back of the room opened and Tony and Susan stepped out. Kat hoped her parents had already been spirited away. She turned and saw several of the student volunteers in their teal uniforms coming in behind Cameron's crew.

Although Tony had only wanted full officers on this detail, clearly he had kept some of the recruits nearby as a reserve. Kat spotted Paul among them as they filtered into the room. She thought he'd be promoted soon. For all his gangly awkwardness, he had a good head on his shoulders. Tony had likely selected the most promising of the trainees for this assignment.

Kat stood to her full height, pulling her charge gently to his feet. Aside from the gash on his head, which had bled freely, and his white pallor, he didn't seem to have any other injuries.

"What's your name?" she asked in a soft voice.

He took a minute to respond. "Ben. Thanks. My glasses?"

Ben might have lost a lot of blood, or he might be in shock, or both. Either way, Kat needed to get him some medical attention. She looked around to see everything was well in hand—the recruits were finding the injured and starting to lead them out of the building. And there were injured.

But she suspected Ben might be worse off than most, so she stopped dithering and gently walked him out of the hall. Outside a full medical triage had been set up. A couple of nurses and some aides were standing at the top of the steps, while more sisters had a tent set up on the grass at the bottom, where a few medical techs and more aides waited next to two ambulances with their back doors open and ready— gasoline rationing didn't apply to them. The sisters had turned out fast and in force.

Kat didn't bother with the nurses on the landing who were trying to sort the wounded as they left the building. She just marched down the steps, almost carrying Ben in her haste. She handed him over to the sisters at the tent, who looked like they might want to object.

Kat spoke first. "He's got a nasty contusion with a laceration. He's lost a lot of blood and he may be in shock. And his name is Ben." And she watched as two aides loaded the boy onto a gurney.

The nurse began checking Ben's vitals, then she ordered him loaded onto the ambulance and taken to the clinic. While this was being done she took Kat by the arm and led her over to one of the folding chairs in the tent, next to a table piled with medical supplies, and started taking her pulse.

"Look here—"

But this time the nurse wouldn't let Kat do the talking. "You didn't let my sisters take a look at you, so be quiet and let me do my job."

Since Kat clearly wouldn't be able to escape the sister, she tried to muster up the patience to wait until the nurse had finished. She hoped to be done and gone before people saw and assumed she was pampering herself. As soon as she was released she jumped to her feet.

As she walked, she rubbed her wrist to check the time—and felt dazed when she saw that barely fifteen minutes had passed since her mom had called the meeting to order. It felt more like a lifetime.

Tony appearing at her elbow also caught her by surprise. "I might've known you'd be the one insisting on putting yourself in harm's way."

Kat made the best attempt at a smile she could manage right then. "It's true I had a bit of a tumble in there."

Tony looked grim. "While I'm glad you're not seriously hurt, Kat, none of my other officers took a beating."

"Hardly a beating, Boss. I might have a couple light bruises." Kat walked with Tony out of the way of the oncoming patients. "What about Dad? Caroline and the rest?"

"Your parents and Ms. Belue are fine. I had an evacuation plan all ready. It's my plan for the worst philosophy."

Kat managed a grin. "I like to hope for the best. It's just who I am."

As she said that, Kat's brain finally made a connection it should have long before this. The reason

Councilman Radley had looked familiar to her. He was an older version of that louse who'd caused her all that trouble what now seemed ages ago.

She had never followed up to find out who he was, but she'd wager he was a close relative of the councilman's—a younger brother or a son. Instead of just dealing with the troublemakers as they came, maybe she should be paying more attention to just who wanted to cause trouble and why.

Kat could bring that subject up with Tony later. Right now there was probably work to do, and she'd go ahead and assume the nurse had cleared her for duty. "So, what do you want me to do now, Boss?" Whatever it was, she first had to try and find a pair of glasses.

Chapter 7

Scattering Dust

5:15 p.m. Sunday, December 8th

DAVID grabbed two hotdogs in one hand and saluted Ken with the other. "Sorry to have to eat and run." Though he hadn't done either, yet.

His boss was standing at the grill, scowling as he added more meat to the fire. "You just began sharing Sunday dinners with us."

Indeed, David considered it an honor to be included in the tradition with the rest of Ken's crew, and having to leave so soon was why he'd shown up early to help out with the preparations. Then he'd excused himself on the grounds of a prior commitment he had to keep. The rest of the crew had only just started to drift into Jeff and Sandy's back yard.

The light was now beginning to fade, but David still had the time to try and talk to his boss again. "Boss, about this Colonel Gray..." He trailed off as he saw Ken's face.

His boss waved the hot tongs in the air. "Gray is not your business. There are people who can worry about the man, and if there's anything needing to be done, they can do it."

David nodded in acknowledgement. Thinking the same, he'd told his mother about his suspicions of Gray and Rossiter. At least she'd really listened to him. But she'd told him what he'd expected to hear —that there wasn't much to be done without some kind of evidence.

He'd tried to talk to Ken about it as well, but his boss hadn't wanted to listen. So David would operate by Ken's own motto. He'd do what he believed was right, even if it wasn't his business. Because no one else seemed to be taking care of it, he had to do what he could himself.

He smiled and turned and walked away. As he left the yard, he looked back at the tableau behind him—his boss flipping burgers on the grill with the crew gathering around, and Sandy coming out with two giant pitchers of iced tea. All so normal that it seemed completely unreal. Everyone kept going on with life as usual, as much as they could anyway, as if nothing were different.

David felt like his whole life had changed. The compound had been sealed and they were all under threat. He'd set aside his studies to accept his new responsibilities—and everything just continued to keep changing. He'd given up Sunday dinners at home so he could partake with Ken and the rest, but for now he was abandoning that, too. If his life kept turning around, soon it would turn upside down.

He sighed and hurried down the sidewalk. He hadn't wanted to disappoint Ken any more than he had to, so he'd left the timing close. Now he needed to rush. He trotted along, wolfing down the freshly charred hotdogs even though they might be his last. Next week they'd likely be reduced to barbequing tilapia filets or frozen frog legs.

By now, Sgt. Rossiter would be eating his own dinner at the Guard HQ, presuming he stuck to the schedule he'd followed all week. This was the first time David would try to follow him on a Sunday. If he managed to arrive in time to position himself for trailing the sergeant when he left, if he left, maybe he'd have more success tonight.

It had been a frustrating week. As David strode down the sidewalk, he reflected on how little he had accomplished in his effort to find evidence of what Rossiter was doing. Which might be expected, since he had no real idea what he was doing himself. He consoled himself with the fact that others also knew of his suspicions—he'd talked with Lt. Henson, his mother and somewhat with Ken. It wasn't all on his shoulders.

Still, the lieutenant hadn't sounded as if he was prepared to actually do anything, and Ken certainly wouldn't. David's mother had said there was little she *could* do, but she'd report what he'd confided in her to whomever might be responsible for dealing with it, for whatever good that might do. But David didn't feel that was enough.

So he'd refrained from telling her he intended to investigate on his own, though he'd no clue what he might be able to do, or how. The FURCSnet restricted access to the personnel records, and without the ability to connect to the real web, any details about Rossiter and Gray that were surely out there somewhere were beyond David's reach. And he couldn't very well go around asking questions.

He turned the corner onto the main thorough-fare and looked carefully both ways before crossing to the other side, even though the street was empty of any hint of traffic. Everyone was saving their gas for the day the gates might open again. He hustled toward the perimeter, checking his watch and praying he'd be in time to catch the sergeant.

After considering the problem, David had realized his best, if not only hope of finding something was to follow the sergeant again—but he dared not trail the man around in the daytime. If Sgt. Rossiter had spotted him that first time, the man could've chalked it up to coincidence. He should have if he'd heard about David's lunch with Lt. Henson.

But David couldn't risk being noticed anymore, even if he'd been willing to skip out on work, which he wasn't. Thankfully, the job chugged along more smoothly now. He'd even got his crew to know what they were doing, well enough that he didn't have to supervise them so much, and he could sneak in doing some more of the work himself. So he didn't feel bad when he clocked out with his crew instead of working late.

Since he couldn't follow Rossiter around in the day, he would have to do it at night, and that meant changing his schedule. So for the past week, he'd gone home for an early supper in the kitchen, chatting with Crystal. Then he'd take a short nap before heading out to find the sergeant.

On Monday, David had tried chatting with the not particularly pleasant guards on duty, and with a little patience he'd teased out what he needed—the fact that Rossiter regularly took his evening repast around dusk in the cafeteria at the Guard HQ. And that gave him his starting point.

He didn't know much about how to go around following someone, but Monday evening he'd found a spot in the shadow of a nearby building where he thought he'd be able to spy the sergeant coming out of the HQ without being observed himself. David did see the man when he left, but tailing him turned out to be more difficult.

From the beginning he'd practiced prudence, preferring the risk of losing the sergeant to the risk of being discovered. And he did end up losing him. Six nights in a row and he hadn't found the proof he sought—but since he always lost track of the man, David didn't know what he might be missing.

But after last night, he believed there was something to be missed. He was considering whether he might need a new strategy if tonight's effort failed when he caught sight of Rossiter leaving the back of the HQ and heading toward the barracks. Once the sergeant was inside, David sauntered over to a different shadow that offered a better vantage point.

So far, Rossiter had stuck to his routine. If he continued as usual, the sergeant would soon reappear. If he bedded down for the night though, David would be standing around for a long time.

He wished he could check his watch. But he worried that the bright illumination would give him away. It wasn't long, though, before Rossiter came out carrying his duffle bag, as he had on three previous occasions. Each evening that the sergeant had taken his bag before, he'd then taken the tram to the Rec Center.

Not wanting to take any chances, David waited until he was sure Rossiter was headed for the stop just shy of the main thoroughfare. Then he walked off in the opposite direction.

One of his preparations had been memorizing the tram stations and schedule, and as soon as he was too far away for the sergeant to notice, David started his sprint. He reached the station outside the Tech Center before the tram. A gaggle of students waited there, and his breathless arrival might have attracted attention from other folk, but these people were so absorbed in their own discussions that David might as well have been invisible.

And they themselves made good camouflage. David circled around the group to position himself for snagging a seat on the back car, where the crowd should shield him from Rossiter's notice. He only hoped he'd be able to watch the sergeant as the man got on and off.

The tram pulled to a stop and the students all rushed on board, cramming together in the middle segments. Rossiter was waiting at the next station. He jumped onto the front car, avoiding the students like the plague and making things easier for David. For the moment.

Snaking through the compound, and stopping several times, it took the tram nearly half an hour to reach the Rec Center, where the sergeant did indeed jump off. David waited for everyone else to disembark, only hopping off himself when the tram began to pull away. *So far, so good.* The next part, though, caused him to sweat just thinking about it.

Three times he had followed Rossiter here, and each time he'd been forced to make a difficult decision about what to do. The massive square edifice was three stories high and filled with an assortment of rooms equipped for all different kinds of sports and exercise. David didn't come here, because he got more exercise than he wanted at work, but it was one of the few places where residents of all stripes mingled freely.

The first time, David had presumed the crowd would help conceal him from the sergeant, but he hadn't considered how effectively it would also hide the man he was following. Keeping a safe distance from Rossiter as he entered, he then found himself in a futile search. He'd wandered through the building aimlessly, finding Eric and his toadies pumping iron, but hope as he might he found not a glimpse of the sergeant. Eventually he had given up and gone home.

The second time, David had followed Rossiter into the place as close behind as he dared, and he'd kept track of the man for a while but still lost him in the crowd. If Rossiter had come for an illicit rendezvous, David despaired of actually finding out. Then yesterday evening, David had changed tactics once again. If he couldn't catch the sergeant having a clandestine meeting with someone, maybe he could at least find out where the man went next, and maybe that would give him a new lead to follow.

So after Rossiter and his duffle bag entered the building, David had searched for a convenient spot to surveil the main entrance and wait for the man to leave. But he never saw the sergeant leave.

He had waited until they closed up at eleven and cleared everyone out of the building, and there had been no sign of Rossiter. He'd considered different explanations for how that might have happened. He couldn't believe the sergeant had bribed someone to let him stay, since it would only draw attention, and achieved nothing as far as David could imagine.

From his previous visits, he knew there were a couple other exits, but those were inconvenient and meant only for staff—which left one obvious conclusion in David's mind. Whatever business Rossiter might've had inside the building, he'd left by a discreet exit, to avoid being followed. David sweated now because *that* made him nervous.

It made him feel sure the sergeant was engaged in something, something which he would take great pains to hide from prying eyes. It raised a question, though—whether Rossiter suspected someone was following him, or whether he was taking such precautions as a matter of routine. Either possibility was disturbing.

The first one suggested the sergeant might have twigged to David's tail. The second possibility implied Rossiter was up to something just as serious as David's most dire speculations.

Tonight might be the best opportunity to find out what that was. Last night, David had returned home late—and feeling pretty pale at the implications of his own thoughts. He'd found his mother waiting up for him. She had seemed a bit blanched from her own ordeal—there'd been a near riot at the Community Hall and she'd been worried about him. She didn't want him wandering about late at night. David didn't want that either, and if tonight didn't pan out, perhaps he'd be able to think of a different avenue of investigation.

He'd planned out what to do after morning services. He'd filled up at lunch with his mom since he intended skipping dinner with Ken's crew. After he finished eating, he'd traveled to the Rec Center and searched thoroughly to make sure there were only the two exits besides the main entrance. Then he'd scoped out a good spot where he could keep an eye on both of those staff doors, a warehouse with poor exterior lighting.

David headed there now for his stakeout. He didn't know how soon Rossiter might emerge, so he prepared for a long wait. He leaned up against the building, and after propping up the wall for several minutes, his eyes snapped open and he realized he'd fallen asleep—at least he hoped it hand only been a few minutes. He didn't dare check his watch.

Long days of hard work and long nights of this business and precious little sleep were all catching up with him, and now he could've missed his best opportunity for all he knew. He pinched himself. He breathed deeply of the crisp night air, leaning forward away from the building. He had to do this right.

He stretched a little to stay limber and twisted his head from side to side. Easing the crick from his neck was how he happened to catch a glimpse of the shadowy figure of Rossiter in the distance. He *had* missed the man.

David plunged into the night after the sergeant. The man must have slipped out the far staff door while David was nodding off—and he wasn't carrying his duffel bag anymore. David thanked God that he'd noticed Rossiter's shape in the darkness when he had—especially since he'd been looking for the silhouette of a man with a duffel. His curiosity was piqued by that absence, but he'd have to ponder that problem later.

As he scanned the night for the sergeant, he began to worry that he'd lost the man already. Again.

David slowed his pace and squinted into the darkness, and as his eyes searched so did his mind, for some idea of where Rossiter might be headed.

When the sergeant had left the Rec Center, he would have believed himself free of observation. So he would have had no reason to disguise his direction. And he'd headed south.

So David strolled along that same way, trying to think, to test the possibilities while looking keenly into the shadows. The path he took would lead past the back entrance of the Community Hall. Plenty of important people there, but as early in the evening as it still was, it would likely be busy, too busy.

When David approached the building, he saw that indeed several people came and went, and for that very reason he doubted the sergeant had gone inside. Too public for anything private. He kept his head low, though, and avoided making eye contact with anyone as he walked past casting casual looks about. He didn't see Rossiter, who was probably far ahead of him by now.

He had likely missed his chance. He continued to search, but found no indication of the sergeant's presence anywhere. The walkway he trod turned to follow a residential street that would curve around toward the main thoroughfare and end up near the main gate and the Guard HQ. Rossiter could be headed back to the barracks.

David considered a more promising possibility. This more upscale section of the community housed most of the prominent residents, including his own mother and the director himself. Of course, if he discovered the sergeant meeting secretly with the director, then David would know he had got hold of the wrong end of the stick altogether. He snickered silently at the thought.

However, other leaders of FURC and the wider community lived around here. Any of which might make sense as a possible conspirator, but unless he happened to come upon Rossiter sneaking in or out of one of these homes, David had no clue who that might be. So he just walked on. Eventually, though, if he just kept going on, he'd only finish up where he began.

He saw no point to traveling that far. Even if he did see the sergeant returning to the barracks, that wouldn't tell David anything. He resisted admitting defeat. He slowed his pace and started to meander through the neighborhood, hoping for something.

He saw his mother's house and veered in a wide circle around it. He didn't want to answer awkward questions about what he was doing, when he wasn't sure he knew himself right now. He thought of his comfortable bed and the rest he clearly needed.

He stopped and knelt. He pretended to tie his bootlaces while he considered. He could continue wandering around the neighborhood in the hope he chanced to see Rossiter—and make himself look suspicious in the process. David thought he'd best give up, go home and get some sleep.

He began to rise and head back when he froze. *Sgt. Rossiter.* David witnessed the sergeant sneak out someone's back door and slink away—off into the night. And it was David's own home Rossiter had left.

He remained stuck there in a half crouch, heart racing as a sudden image of his mother lying on the kitchen floor in a pool of blood leaped into his head. Rossiter's shadow was already disappearing across the next lawn. David would hunt the man down like the animal he was if David's mom had been hurt.

He almost took right off after the man. Then his irrational fear receded and the moment of rage gave way. David stood slowly and calmly considered the facts. Lights shined in a few of the windows, and he doubted the sergeant would have burgled an occupied house. He waited a few minutes. A silhouette moved in the kitchen, and though it was small and shapeless behind the curtains, it comforted David with a feeling of normality.

Then he realized that the light had been out in the utility room when the sergeant slipped out the back. Rossiter could have turned it out himself to effect a stealthy departure. What it suggested however was the same thing David had been suspecting all along, why he had been following the man in the first place. The sergeant had been meeting someone on the sly.

David turned his watch light on and checked the time. A little after seven and Crystal had probably left for her aerobics class, leaving his mother alone in the house. But it was inconceivable that his mom would have had an illicit rendezvous with Rossiter. Perhaps Crystal was the figure he saw, still there cleaning up in the kitchen after dinner and not yet having departed—because she'd needed to talk to the sergeant first.

David had to know. He circled back around to the front of the house and up to the door, where he hesitated a moment before unlocking. He met the housekeeper in the foyer.

Crystal had her purse in hand and started when she saw him entering. "We didn't expect you to be back this early, David." She smiled. "I hope you had a good time. Your mother's in her study, working I think, and not wanting to be disturbed." She sidled past him on her way to the door. "I'm late for my exercise, or I'd stay and talk a while."

She waved at him on her way out. David smiled and nodded and waved back. At least he had a new lead to follow.

Chapter 8

Conspiracy Theories

10:40 p.m. Wednesday, December 12th

KAT jogged down the sidewalk, Paul matching her pace in the cart as it hummed alongside on the main thoroughfare. Paul had been promoted to an officer and not before time. Hope stared across Paul at Kat, while Ben scanned the night behind them from the back bench.

Kat hadn't been able to find Ben's glasses, but the sisters had went ahead and lasered his actual lenses so he no longer needed any specs.

Apparently Ben was some kind of boy genius, the freaky kind. He'd been exempted from the work requirement Kat had believed all FedU students had to fulfill—she'd never even heard of an exemption until she'd found out about Ben. But now the boy had volunteered for Security, and Kat worried he'd imprinted on her like a baby chick. Though with or without glasses he looked more like a lost puppy.

Hope chirped, "I can't believe it." She kept staring at Kat while she asked Paul, "How many miles has she run now?" She continued without waiting for an answer. "It's so impressive. Maybe I should give it a try."

Kat glanced over without breaking stride. "Perhaps you'd best start with something easier. I could show you a few simple exercises to practice."

Hope seemed a little relieved. "That sounds like a good idea. Maybe later."

Kat just nodded and returned her eyes to scanning the darkness ahead. Hope's admiration was misplaced. Kat knew she'd let herself get too far out of shape, and this was no time for her to be at less than peak performance. So she'd started using the late evening patrols to get in a little running.

After the weekend, the compound residents had tamped down their frustrations, but she thought it only a matter of time before things heated up again. For now though, relative calm had descended. And it gave her time to exercise and a chance to keep Ben and Hope out of harm's way.

Tony had changed the policy now that he'd promoted several new officers. Every patrol required a pair of officers and at least one of the recruits along for the experience, though Kat thought their presence more a hindrance than a help. By taking both Ben and Hope along with her, she could keep a close eye on Ben and prevent anyone else being saddled with Hope.

There was nothing wrong with Hope, who was quite nice. She wasn't cut out to be an officer, however, and continuing to take her on patrol wouldn't change that. The girl was better suited to the role of safety aide that student volunteers used to play, and there was still need for that kind of help—despite how much life in the community had changed.

They should be separating the volunteers into support roles and officer trainees rather than treating them all as potential officers. Then Hope could stay safe in the HQ taking care of the office routine. Kat ought to suggest something of the sort to Tony, and not just because she herself hated office work.

She saw the perimeter wall up in the distance, and the fence beyond. No use patrolling there with all the guards around. She signaled to Paul and ran faster as she rounded a corner onto one of the residential streets. Then she slowed her pace until he caught up with her.

She checked the time. "We'd better head back." The two trainees went off shift at eleven, and Paul and Kat should take their breaks.

Kat wouldn't have much of a break, though. She thought of Saturday night's brouhaha and still had trouble believing good people could lose control like that. She'd come to suspect someone might've been pushing their buttons. And when she'd returned to the office exhausted in the wee hours, she'd immediately pulled the arrest records for the night of the twenty-seventh and read the details of the trouble-makers she'd taken down. Then she'd started going back over the incident logs for the previous weeks.

Tony had discovered her with her head lying on the conference room table, sleeping, and he'd recognized right away what she'd been up to. He'd simply shaken his head and suggested she go home to bed and work on her 'little project' later.

Kat jogged around another corner to steer them back in the direction of headquarters. She was starting to tire now. It would be good to get off her feet for a little while—though it would be better still if she weren't going to exercise her brain pouring over personnel records.

Tony had encouraged her to continue digging through the records, investigating. Which was unfortunate, since going through all those files hadn't produced anything other than eyestrain.

Kat still suspected some agitator might be provoking tensions within the community, but with no progress to show for her efforts, she'd been prepared to leave off trying to find out who. Then Tony had recommended that she examine *all* the residents' records—students and teachers and researchers. The administrative staff and technicians, laborers and tradesmen, even the guards and security staff themselves. The mere thought was enough to make Kat groan. But she hadn't wanted to disappoint her boss, so she'd persevered.

She had been spending her breaks in a secure suite, combing through everyone's files even though she didn't know what she was looking for. Indeed, she had even less of an idea now what she was trying to find than when she'd started. She wasn't particularly looking forward to her break.

Kat *did* eagerly anticipate her next patrol—after midnight, when she planned to take Susan with her and no trainees. At that time of night, she made the trainees stick to the office—Tony's new policy notwithstanding. Despite the recent relative calm that had descended, in the darkest hours of night, there would be malefactors making mischief somewhere out there, and Kat would find them. She was developing a nose for sniffing them out.

Susan made a good partner for dealing with the miscreants, too. She might not have Kat's reflexes, but she didn't need them with her level head, steady hand, and practical approach to taking care of business. They complemented each other quite well.

Kat rued not being able to skip ahead to the fun part, the patrol that promised at least the potential for danger and some much needed practice, but she needed to get Ben and Hope squared away first. And then spend an hour staring at a screen. She'd have to drink plenty of coffee to keep her awake—if Tony came by to check on her progress, she'd rather be found hard at work than drooling on the table.

With her mind drifting as she ran, Kat ended up back at headquarters in no time. She asked Paul to drop Ben and Hope off at the dorms before putting the cart away and taking his break. She could trust Paul to make the short trip back alone without getting into any trouble, but she didn't want to take the chance with Ben and Hope walking that far on their own. She promised the pair she'd log them out and waved goodbye.

Kat watched the three of them trundle off across the grass in the buggy and sighed before walking her weary legs into the office. She nodded to the girl at the duty desk and let herself be buzzed through the gate. Tony's office door was ajar with light spilling out, telling her the man was in and working when he should be resting. *He tries to do too much.*

Tony had been spending long hours training the new recruits so they'd have enough officers—not to mention going out at night to patrol on his own, in defiance of his own regulations. *Men.*

Kat didn't feel up to remonstrating with Tony about that now. Instead she turned and trudged up the stairs to the second floor and down the hall to the innocuously named Resource Room, where all the classified information resided. Past that, at the end of the corridor were Tony's private rooms. She knew of no one else who lived where they worked, unless she counted her father, but that was a different situation.

She stood at the door and stared at the security key in the palm of her hand. Part of the reason she couldn't disappoint Tony was because he had placed so much trust in her. Kat plugged the key into her FURCS pad, then inserted the key into the lock and used her fingerprint to open the door and slip in.

She passed through the tiny office itself and into the kitchenette. She started a pot of coffee brewing right away, and not simply to help her stay awake. This place felt colder than the rest of the building. Cold and isolated.

She returned to the office with a full, steaming mug, wondering why the FURC didn't use security cameras. Though if they'd had them, she'd have found herself spending hours staring at video footage instead of, or in addition to, all these snarled computer files.

Either way would be the same tortuous tedium. She set her coffee down and then settled herself in the comfy chair, grabbing the workpad that held all the residents' information in thoroughly compiled digital files. Kat had begun by attempting to read through every single record in a methodical fashion. Though with thousands of people's history to sift through, she'd become bored fast.

Then she had decided to look for connections. She'd started with Councilman Radley and his son Brandon, then moved on to Brandon's friends and their friends, their teachers, and their colleagues. She'd studied the files on Radley's employees who lived or worked in the community, mostly researchers and technicians. Finding nothing of note, she'd given up on that entire line of inquiry.

Kat had found herself reading through Ben Laskey's slim but interesting record and proceeded to skim through the rest of her co-workers. She felt a bit guilty about that. But she justified her curiosity by telling herself anyone working in Security ought to be thoroughly vetted.

Though Tony must've gone through these same files himself before accepting any of them—still he'd given them all to her and suggested a close examination. Kat wondered if there existed any reason for that assignment, apart from the whole thing being a bizarre form of punishment.

Tonight she'd take a different tack entirely. She tried to think who in the community would be most unsuspected. She decided to treat those people to some extra scrutiny, but as she was looking around for such unlikely prospects, Kat came to a startling realization. And quickly filed it away for later.

She opened up contractor Ken Cameron's file and started reading, and at least it was entertaining. The man had certainly led an interesting life. Two tours in the army and he'd only made sergeant, but he'd served in both the Egyptian War and Second Korean Conflict, short as those were. He'd left the military to start his own contracting business. And occasionally he taught marksmanship seminars at Quantico, which was quite startling—the man must be quite the expert.

Kat caught her thoughts short again. Cameron had taught at Quantico during the same period her father and Tony had been there, when the two men had become fast friends. Tony had been FBI at the time. Kat had never been told why her father had been there, only that she wasn't supposed to know about it and had better not breathe a word of it.

She had no reason to think either Tony or her dad had met Ken Cameron, simply because they'd been there at the same time. As far as she knew, the contractor was only a casual acquaintance of either man, yet her mind leapt to the notion of the three men as a secret cabal—no doubt engaged in some kind of complicated conspiracy.

Kat mentally pinched herself and reached for more coffee. Wading through these files looking for suspicious connections must be warping her brain. She'd start seeing conspiracies everywhere unless she stopped. She did have legitimate questions to ask, but she would take those to Tony later.

She skimmed over some more files. Lt. Henson in the Guards had gone over to the British Isles to serve in the SAS during the Difficulties. No details of what he did there, but hardly any of that had been documented. Alice Kittner had been quite the radical before entering academia. Somehow the woman had avoided jail. Jeffrey Minchin had earned three unrelated degrees in college and now worked as a landscaper.

Kat discarded the notion of reading through her mother's records, since she was already developing quite the headache. She flipped through a few random records, which might be as helpful as anything. She stretched in the chair and thought about taking a short nap—maybe it *was* time to approach Tony.

She downed the rest of her coffee and firmly pushed herself out of the chair. A deep breath and she clutched the pad to her chest, marching out of the room and down the stairs. The resolve did more to stimulate her than the coffee.

She marched straight into Tony's office without knocking, but the man only lifted an eyebrow at her.

"Boss," Kat started, trying to control her tone, "this is a huge waste of time."

Tony straightened in his chair. "Shut the door."

She turned and closed the door behind her and returned her glare to Tony.

The man smiled. "Okay, Kat, now rant all you want. The room's soundproofed."

She clenched her jaw and took another deep breath before starting again. "How am I meant to find anything in here?" She gestured with the large pad. "Anything that might give an inkling of who would be deliberating stirring the pot, or why?"

"Kat, that's sensitive information. That pad is supposed to stay locked up in the Resource Room."

She ignored his chiding. "What did you think I would find? That Councilman Radley is a commercial fishing magnate. Maybe he's rubbed shoulders with Governor Roberts, or greased the man's palms to help his business, but even if that kind of information was in here—" Kat paused to glare, "which it's not—how would that prove anything?"

Tony sighed. "How would I know what in the world you should be looking for? It was your idea in the first place."

She ignored that. "What *is* a commercial fisherman doing here anyway? We're as far from either coast as you could get. Maybe that's suspicious, but I just don't know." She set the pad down on his desk and leaned forward on her fists. "I've examined the connections until I'm seeing potential conspiracies behind every corner, but I've not found one solid hint. There are plenty of red herrings, though. All these people categorized under 'no particular function'—do you know how long it was before I figured out that was the classification for the family members of FURC employees."

Tony leaned back in his chair. "You were the one, Kat, who thought someone might be intentionally agitating residents, making trouble. I was just trying to help, giving you access to those files."

Kat straightened with a smile and crossed her arms. "Help?" She stared Tony straight in the eye. "Then tell me why two particular files are missing from what you gave me. Neither Chief Gray's nor the deputy director's records are in there."

Neither her father's nor Tony's were as well, but that hadn't surprised her. That the other two individual's files should also have been removed did.

Tony shrugged. "Miles vouched for Ms. Belue. Without reservation."

Kat's gaze didn't shift an inch. "That was only half an answer." She continued to wait.

After a few moments, Tony relented. "Lock the doors, Kat."

She grinned in triumph as she crossed the room and turned both deadbolts. She returned to stand before her boss, expectant. Tony took a long swig of water and made her wait, but Kat was prepared to be patient.

Tony scratched the stubble on his chin. "You might as well sit down."

She pulled one of the chairs up close and sat down on the edge of the seat. "Now, what is it you didn't want me to see?"

Tony worked his jaw for a long moment, and she knew she had him on the defensive. "Okay, but this is strictly between us. Highly confidential."

Kat lifted an eyebrow and wondered if he really thought she might need that warning. *How careless does he think I am?* "Chief Gray?"

"Gray was a colonel in the Florida Army National Guard before he was forced to retire. Before that he was thick with Governor Roberts."

Kat sat back in her chair. "Then he's an enemy agent?" Her mind raced as she imagined the possible ramifications.

"Don't jump to conclusions." Tony shook his finger at her. "Despite current conditions, we're not dealing with embittered enemies. It's politics."

Kat snorted at that. "There's a difference?"

Tony frowned back at her. "Yes, and you need to appreciate the subtleties. The FURC construction was a huge project with lots of money flowing into the state and plenty of opportunities, but Governor

Roberts was shut out of the process. On purpose. But powerful men like him don't take that kind of thing lying down, and the governor somehow managed to foist the recently retired Gray on us. In spite of the man's record."

"Which you don't want me to read."

Tony shook his head. "I do now." He grabbed the large workpad she had dropped on his desk and began fiddling.

Kat watched for a minute, unwilling to leave the topic there. "And? The man's a mole."

"We know Gray was placed here to be the governor's eyes and ears, but that doesn't mean he must be some kind of enemy agent."

Kat goggled. "The man could be up to anything. And he's got command of the Guards, all of the external security. Aren't you doing anything?"

"Certainly. I've been trying to surveil the man's activities as much as I can. And I have a little help there. But we don't want to spook Chief Gray into taking any precipitate action."

"What's that supposed to mean?"

"With what we can glean of the man's character, we don't think Gray will make a move without instructions from Roberts, which he can't get because of the communications blackout. But if Chief Gray starts thinking that we're coming after him? Read his record, Kat, and tell me what you think."

Kat found she had leaned forward again to the edge of her seat as she was listening. She started tapping her foot against the desk, thinking fast.

"It's been almost three weeks, Tony. In that time the governor could have found a way to get a message in to Gray, or the man could have hatched some plan of his own, if he's concerned about his position here."

"It's possible."

"Does Gray know he was foisted on my father against my dad's will? He should be worried. I've not read his record yet, I know, but the man must have considered the situation he's in with the compound being sealed. Started to make some kind of calculations. We need to know more."

Tony nodded. "Sure. We want all the intelligence on Gray we can get. We've got to be careful how we go about gathering that information is all."

Kat moistened her lips. "Do you have any other suspects? If the governor managed to plant one of his people here, there could be more. Working with Chief Gray. Have you considered that?"

Tony nodded again. "I've got my doubts about a number of people. One is a Sgt. Rossiter. Gray uses him all the time as an errand boy, but we've other grounds for suspicion. I've got my intuition about some others, but no evidence. There's still a lot we don't know, as you said."

Kat frowned. "Then we need to find out."

Tony scratched the stubble on his chin, looking at Kat for a long moment. "Would you be interested in a dangerous new assignment?"

Kat grinned. "What do you think?"

Tony frowned. "I mean making yourself into a target. I'd be making you an obvious spy. It's something only you could do."

Kat was intrigued. "But I thought you wanted to avoid provoking him? Leave him complacent."

Tony smiled. "As you said, he's probably worried about his position already. You'll be something he'll think he can handle, so he'll not be paying attention to what he should. It means being a decoy, as well as a target."

Kat would rather take down Chief Gray herself, but she'd settle for this. "It'll still be more interesting than trawling through those blasted files."

Tony handed over the secured workpad. "Why do you imagine you can get away from them? Study Gray. Learn about the rest of the guards. Take this seriously."

"Boss, you worry too much." Kat grinned even wider. "I'll do what needs to be done."

Chapter 9

Clear as Mud

7:10 p.m. Friday, December 13th

DAVID drained the last drop of lemonade from his glass and gazed down at the empty plate. He would never have thought fish that hadn't been fried could taste that good. Especially tilapia. Whatever else Crystal might or might not be, she was an incredible cook. It must be the Scandinavian blood.

Though David was no longer sure he could believe anything of what Crystal had said about who she was. All their little chats had become suspect. It'd been awkward enough talking to her when she was an attractive woman who lived and worked in his own home. For the past several days whenever they'd conversed, he'd tried to think of little ways to trip her up, find something inconsistent in her life story. But once again, David was unsure how to go about it. He just felt his way along slow and careful, and discovered nothing.

He sat alone in the dining room. His mom had come home for dinner, ate with rapid precision, and retreated to her study to work. Crystal would be in the kitchen still. David wiped his mouth and picked up his dishes and carried them in to her.

Crystal took the dishes, smiled at him, and added them to the pile she was already washing. "You enjoyed the fish, yes?"

David smiled at the back of her head. "Indeed I did. Good thing, too, since we'll likely be eating a lot more of it. I suppose you learned how to cook that way back in Michigan."

"Minnesota." She frowned over her shoulder at him. "I swear you don't listen to a thing I say."

David sighed. He feared he wasn't being subtle enough. Crystal wasn't stupid, and if she *was* some kind of mole, he needed to watch his step.

"What I *don't* understand is where you get the lemons to make lemonade."

Crystal focused on the dishes and didn't bother to look at him as she responded. "Silly David, who uses real lemons anymore?"

He was still trying to think of something else to say when she finished drying the last of the dishes and put it away in the drainer. Crystal smiled at him again as she left the kitchen.

David checked the clock on the wall and knew she wouldn't be wasting any time, and he'd best not either. He heard her rapid ascent up the stairs, in a rush to get to her aerobics class. *Supposedly.*

David went straight into the hall and rapped on the study door. He waited only a moment, entering as his mother turned off her workpad and set it on the top of her desk. She swiveled around to face him and give him her undivided attention.

"Mom, Crystal's finished cleaning up and about to head out for her exercise. I though I'd go out and have a little walk myself. See if I can find anyone I know." That was the truth, just not the way it might sound to his mother. "Who knows, I might crash at my dorm room, if I'm out late. So don't worry. You don't mind if I abandon you here?"

She shook her head. "I'll be fine. I've got plenty of work to do, anyway, so I don't need any company. Stay out as long as you like." She looked at him for a long minute, frowning. "I hope you get a chance to relax some. You look tired. I know you're working hard, David, but make sure you get plenty of rest."

He thought that ironic coming from her as she sat in her study on a Friday evening, no doubt planning to work late into the night. As was he. Well, neither of them was likely getting enough sleep. If she worried about him, though, he worried as much about her.

David nodded at his mom. "Make sure you get plenty of rest yourself."

He closed the study door behind him as he left and then stood silent in the hall, listening. After a minute he heard Crystal run down the stairs and out the front door. Now to work. He walked to the back door, slipping out without turning on the light, just as Rossiter had.

He circled around toward the front of the house and saw Crystal power-walking up the street in the direction of the Community Hall. He trailed behind her at a discreet distance, needing to be extra careful since she would recognize him without difficulty, but he was still able to follow her with ease. In addition to her striking blonde hair, she wore a shocking pink exercise outfit—she certainly wasn't trying to avoid attracting attention to herself.

Unlike the sergeant. Rossiter had raised David's suspicions with his behavior, but so far nothing that Crystal said or did had sounded the slightest alarm.

The key must be those duffel bags the sergeant kept dropping off at the Rec Center. The only thing that made sense to David was some kind of handoff. If he could only find out what was being passed between the two, or if he could actually witness something being transferred, he'd have enough for his mom to take to someone. Hopefully tonight he'd get the evidence he'd been looking for.

Then David would talk to his mother. He'd refrained from approaching her about what he'd seen Sunday night. For all he knew, or could prove, Rossiter and Crystal were engaged in a secret romance. Difficult as that was to imagine. And if his mom did share his suspicions, she'd likely not countenance keeping Crystal around. He didn't imagine that his mother would go along with playing a part so he could continue his amateur investigation, and then this promising lead might be lost.

David hoped to follow that lead somewhere tonight. He didn't know where at the Rec Center the sergeant might be leaving that bag, and his efforts to follow the man had proved fruitless. But if he could trail Crystal and she led him to the duffel, perhaps even its contents would be revealed. He still hadn't been able to think what might be inside the bag.

He thought it was smart of them not to hand off whatever it was directly to each other, but he didn't understand why Rossiter had taken the risk of visiting Crystal at the house, if she were supposed to pick up something he left at the Rec Center. He thought he did understand one thing, though. The only use he could see Crystal being, as some kind of agent, was for spying on David's mother—who was, after all, the deputy director.

David had considered searching Crystal's room at their house, but the idea had made him severely uncomfortable. He still only had suspicions and no idea what he would be looking for. It seemed a weak thread upon which to justify invading someone's privacy, no matter how serious the matter might be.

Besides, he doubted she'd be foolish enough to leave anything incriminating in her own room. If she'd hidden something elsewhere in the house, he didn't think he could find it no matter how much he searched. Though with so few avenues of investigation open to him, David had looked through all the common areas of the house. To no avail.

Crystal still had her room at the dorms where she could've stashed something. In fact, she could have hid almost anything anywhere, and since he didn't yet have any idea what it was he was actually hoping to find, he'd finally given up.

He'd thought long and hard before he decided what he'd do next—if he couldn't trust what she'd revealed in their talks, he'd have to independently verify all that he could of everything she'd told him. Which wasn't much.

He'd started by taking a long break on Monday morning and traveling back across the compound so he could follow Crystal when she went to her second job. He'd been there at a quarter 'til ten when she left the house and power-walked over to the Media

Centre. David couldn't get too close to her, but he had managed to see her enter the staff area.

Without an excuse for loitering around inside the building, he'd circled the exterior long enough to make sure she hadn't turned around and left again right away, pulling the same trick as Rossiter. He would've been surprised if she'd lied about something so easily checked. But he'd checked anyway.

Now he was following her again, but hoping for more of a result. Although he could keep the bright pink in sight without a problem, he wished Crystal had taken the tram. His feet could've used the rest. He'd been wearing himself thin between working all day and then trailing people after dark. But if Crystal chose to start her exercise early, then he had little choice if he wanted to make sure she was actually headed where she'd claimed.

David thought she would be. She was being too obvious and too careful to not at least appear to do exactly what she'd said. He watched her walk right past the back of the Community Hall and continue on toward the Rec Center. As expected.

Soon she was making a beeline across the grass and up to the main entrance. He stepped up his own pace. He needed to close the distance between them if he didn't want to lose track of her, even in those bright clothes she was wearing, which wouldn't look as out of place on the inside.

One of the things David didn't know was if there were anyone else involved. If there were, then that person might be around, discreetly watching Crystal or the bag or the drop location. David would need to appear to be about his own business.

He'd act normal. At the same time he also needed to keep a keen eye on Crystal, since he suspected she'd be subtle however she managed the pick-up, that *she* wouldn't appear to be doing anything out of the ordinary.

He stayed close enough to follow her progress through the building with ease. She did stand out from the crowd, even in here. He was able to follow her to the second floor and a mirrored studio where a posted schedule announced aerobics classes and dance lessons. He drifted close to the door and saw her set her water bottle down against a far wall and start doing some light stretches. He blushed and moved on in a hurry.

David hadn't considered the potential for embarrassment, but then he hadn't planned to watch the class anyway. He didn't want to draw attention to himself, and he felt confident Crystal wouldn't be drawing attention to herself by walking out in the middle of the class.

He'd accomplished what he'd intended, though. As he'd gone past, he'd seen the schedule and confirmed that she'd be occupied until almost nine.

Another thing David had failed to consider was the question of what he would do with himself from now until the class finished. He needed to blend in with the rest, but he was far too tired to participate in any of the activities. What he needed was rest. But he wasn't going to get that here, and he had an entire hour to kill.

He wandered back outside. At least the air was cool and crisp and fresh, and it was quiet enough to be restful. He needed sleep, and if he tried propping up a nearby structure, like he had when he'd followed Rossiter the other evening, he'd likely nod off standing up and not wake until morning.

David scratched the underside of his wrist, and the time softly glowed. On Wednesday, he'd taken a long lunch break and went to the FURC clinic and paid a considerable chunk of his meager savings to get the subdermally implanted watch. And it still itched. A trendy gadget he'd realized could come in handy if he continued skulking about in the dark.

He stared at the illuminated numbers for a minute. The tram would soon arrive at the Rec Center station, and he decided to hurry over. He met it as it snaked up to the stop, then clambered on board and let himself relax while the thing whisked him home for a quick nap. As long as he remembered to set an alarm he could catch thirty winks and return for the end of Crystal's class refreshed and ready.

Chapter 9

David hoped and prayed that he would find out something tonight. Anything that would allow him to turn this responsibility over to others and get it out of his own hands. He really wasn't any good at this, and he was getting tired of it.

Even though he'd hesitated at sharing his recent discovery with his mother, he'd needed to inform someone. He'd tried to tell Ken, once again finding his boss uninterested. Lt. Henson had listened as always, but he still didn't think it was enough to take official action. So for now, David still acted alone.

He'd spent some time in the evenings at the student dormitories partly so that he could be truthful with his mother when he said he sometimes crashed there. So she wouldn't be worrying about his activities at night. But while he was around there and at the Student Center, he tried to introduce the subject of Crystal and see if he could hear any gossip about her. Anything concerning her public life that might be at odds with how she represented herself. If he could uncover anything of the sort, it might present him with another lead to follow, but he'd come up empty. As far as he could tell, Crystal was no more or less than who and what she seemed. Clearly this was a job for an expert.

With no success finding out more about Crystal, he'd applied himself to the question of what exactly she might be trying to accomplish by spying on his mother. Despite his mom's position, she was hardly a vital cog in the running of things. It set his mind somewhat at ease to realize that no one would try to sabotage the compound by harming his mother. He kept repeating to himself that they couldn't think to achieve anything by that.

David knew his mom did have access to all sorts of confidential information, but he wasn't sure what all that entailed. But he did know she had the codes for the FURCSnet communications system. If Gray or Rossiter could get ahold of those, they'd be able to contact the governor or his people on the outside to coordinate an attack. There might be other things they could want from his mother, but David doubted there was anything else as potentially valuable from their point of view.

He didn't know how Crystal might be expected to acquire the codes, but she was certainly in a position to try. Or maybe her only job was to report on his mom's schedule. Perhaps she had even come to work for his mother in the first place in order to spy on her. Or maybe they'd found a way to get to her somehow. Regardless, if David determined exactly what they had her doing, he'd stand a better chance of figuring out what he could do to stop them.

His eyes snapped open as the tram lurched forward. Startled out of his troubled thoughts, he saw his stop falling away behind him and his street with it. He jumped off the moving car and fell onto the sidewalk. *So much for not attracting attention.*

David picked himself up, dusted himself off and began walking home—to lie down and get the rest he needed. He was looking forward to his comfortable bed and some real sleep.

He just had to remember to set his alarm. As much as he might need the rest, he couldn't afford missing out on the opportunity tonight presented—but he worried that his lack of sleep was affecting his judgment. He had to be sharp. Which was why he had to take the time for a short nap.

He saw his home ahead in the dark and stopped dead where he stood, knowing now that he must be suffering from severe sleep deprivation—for he was witnessing a furtive figure dressed in a trench coat and sunglasses with a scarf wrapped around their head knocking on the front door. Illuminated by the light of his own front porch. *It's absurd.*

He knew he was losing it when the door opened and the strange shadow slipped inside. David stood there for several minutes as he wondered if he was already asleep in his bed and dreaming all of this. Or maybe he hadn't really woken on the tram, and the thing was still chugging around the compound with his slumbering form aboard.

Then the breeze picked up, and he felt the cool, crisp night air blowing against his skin and through his hair. He began to feel more alert. He took a few deep breaths and then tried to pull his mind out of the quagmire into which it had been sinking.

He wasn't imagining things. Crystal was at the Rec Center doing her aerobics, and David's mother was the only person in their house—except for the mysterious character who'd just entered. Who was definitely not Sgt. Rossiter.

David knew he'd been half out of it when he'd witnessed the unknown person going into his home, but he recalled the height and shape of the person well enough. Taller than the sergeant, they hadn't been as broad as the man, even in the trench coat. He'd gotten a definite impression it was a woman. One who could learn something about stealth from David, as unlikely as that seemed.

Perhaps it was simply a friend of his mother's. However, he knew she discouraged company, especially when she was working, which was most of the time. And he doubted a friend of his mom's would go around exhibiting such bizarre behavior.

As if from habit, he moved into the shadow of the back wall of a neighbor's house and staked out his own front door.

His brain tried to fit the pieces of the puzzle together. He saw an absurd picture of his house as the center of some screwball spy comedy, with Crystal and Sgt. Rossiter engaging in one conspiracy, while his mother and some other woman snuck around in a separate skullduggery.

David wanted to laugh at the thought, but it was just too insane, and he was too tired. He wondered if his mother had encouraged him to stay out so she could have her ridiculous rendezvous. Maybe it was a man after all, and this was a romantic encounter.

David tried to stop speculating. His immediate concern should be that he couldn't go in and take a nap, unless he wanted to risk interrupting whatever was going on. If it was an assignation, he would be deeply embarrassed. If it was a meeting of conspirators—his mind shied away from that idea.

He sighed. He couldn't think of any way he'd be able to get his rest now. He could turn around and head back to the Rec Center and wait there for Crystal's class to finish and continue following her—and he likely should. But he'd been investigating for what felt like ages with few leads and little success, and here was a discovery to be made. Even though he had no clue what this new piece of the puzzle was or how it might relate to anything, he felt compelled to stay and find out.

David's goal now was to identify this unidentified visitor. His mother had admitted the person to the house, so he wasn't worried about her safety. Once he knew who the person was, maybe then he'd understand why they had visited in such a curious manner and what he did need to worry about. He'd find out, if the individual didn't slip quietly out the back in a manner becoming increasingly popular of late.

David waited. Unable to get the rest he wanted, he tried to enjoy the quiet stillness of the night. He hoped the cool breeze would be sufficient refreshment, and that it would help him stay alert. And miraculously he did manage to remain awake—for the twenty minutes it took until the walking mystery left his house, skulking out the front door with the porch light shining down.

David started to smile at that. Then as the bundled figure turned in the light and stepped out into the night, he caught a glimpse and his jaw dropped. It was only a glimpse, and with the sunglasses and scarf obscuring her, he'd be crazy to think he'd seen who he thought, so he set it aside. He'd save thinking for when his brain was firing on all cylinders.

He just followed the figure as they went. He'd need to confirm their identity one way or another, if he could.

If he *could* find out who this was, then he could return to trailing Crystal with one discovery already in his pocket. Then perhaps he could go get some sleep.

It was a short walk. The person he tailed strode straight across several lawns and right up to another house in the same neighborhood. He knew to whom the place belonged, and because his mom had told him all about the situation, he even knew who was living there right now.

He should've known he couldn't have mistaken those red curls and that distinctive chin, even in the most fleeting glance. It made perfect sense and no sense at all at the same time. David knew Caroline Sanderson was the sort of important leader in the community his mother would naturally have dealings with, but not in this cloak and dagger fashion. He also knew that the woman was a dogged critic of the administration.

He'd achieved his goal. But he no longer felt up to returning to the Rec Center. He'd made his discovery and identified the unknown quantity, and he could follow this lead, pursue this puzzle later. Now he needed some sleep.

So David turned around and headed for home and his bed. He might have preferred his bed at the dorm, but that was far and the house was close. As he stumbled along, his mind spun.

He had a vague thought that he shouldn't be trying to think, but it got lost among the puzzle pieces flying around in his brain. Crystal worked first for his mom, and then got a second job working as an assistant to Caroline Sanderson, but that wasn't the only connection between the two women.

David had witnessed both Sgt. Rossiter and Caroline sneaking out of his mother's house, and he was forced to wonder if the two surreptitious visits were somehow related. He'd assumed the sergeant had been meeting Crystal, but it could have been David's mom, or even both women.

He had a difficult time seeing his mother as a part of whatever might involve those other people. There'd be no need to spy on her if she was a part of it. Neither would they need to find a way to get the access codes from her.

And he'd forgotten about Chief Gray. He had a difficult time imagining Gray as the puppet master pulling all these strings, especially if David's mother was to be one of the puppets. If he were to look for the brains behind the conspiracy, his mother made a more logical suspect. *I don't believe it.*

He must be missing something. His mother and Caroline, Crystal and Rossiter and Gray. The names kept turning in his head, trying to fit together, whirling around with everything he'd seen and heard.

David barely knew he'd come home when he realized he was climbing the stairs. He walked to his room in a daze. And as his head hit the pillow, he thought he saw the whole picture, but it was already escaping into the empty black.

Chapter 10

Not So Covert Action

5:55 p.m. Saturday, December 14th

KAT shoved back her chair as she stood, grabbing her tray from the table. She was enjoying the food here, and the company, and it compensated a little for her lack of progress.

She grinned around at the guards she'd shared her meal with. "Don't worry. I'm not telling anyone how good the cooking is. Or what kind of stories you guys have been making up."

They all smiled at her and offered mock salutes as she turned to leave. Thankfully she'd not had any trouble making friends with the rank-and-file, even after her horrible blunder that first day. Frustrated that she couldn't find Sgt. Rossiter anywhere, she'd insisted on conducting a thorough inspection of the guards' barracks, in a manner that had likely come across as high-handed and insulting.

Perhaps the men had been embarrassed. Aside from a few clerks, there weren't any other females around—and none among the guards themselves. But Kat had smoothed things over afterwards.

She had hoped to find Sgt. Rossiter here putting on his feed bag, since that seemed to be his routine, but once again he was absent on some vague errand. She'd made the best of the situation and enjoyed a satisfying dinner with some of the regular guards. They'd probably return for seconds, but she wanted to move on. In more ways than one.

Aside from the simple job Tony had handed her, she was also determined to find out something useful on her own. As long as she was here, she might as well try. Since she was already spending her time getting to know the guards, she figured careful observation would go a long way. And maybe it would, eventually, but she was getting tired of waiting.

Outside the cafeteria, Kat stalked down the hall toward Chief Gray's office. She called him 'Colonel' —in public at least, because everyone else did, and she had ruffled enough feathers as it was. But the runaround Gray had been giving her over the past three days only confirmed the initial impression of the man she'd gotten from reading his file.

Kat thought Tony should be less worried about Chief Gray being pressured into precipitate action, and more concerned about how to get the man to take any action at all. Surely Gray would do more harm to the compound through sheer laziness than he ever could by actually trying.

She ignored the aide sitting outside Gray's office and walked right in without knocking. Despite his position and former rank, she didn't have to be polite in private, or put up with any nonsense out of him, and he knew that. Or he should.

Chief Gray raised his chin from his chest as she entered, then slowly smiled at her. Kat was at a loss for words. The man had clearly been napping.

Aside from what she considered his general incompetence, Gray even looked his name. This was one old mare that needed to be put out to pasture. She wasn't sure why it hadn't been done yet.

"Well, where's Rossiter now?" Kat deliberately dropped the deference she showed him in front of the guards. "I've had a chance to evaluate your other two sergeants." But she hadn't even met Rossiter yet, and Tony had told her to check him out first.

Gray wiped his mouth with a handkerchief and returned it to his pocket. "Excuse me, Miss Miles. I'm always a bit drowsy after my supper."

Kat kept her jaw firmly shut to avoid making a rejoinder. She also refrained from pulling her own hair out. She would not allow this sorry excuse for a leader get to her. "Rossiter?"

"Oh. I sent him off to check on something. The work on the perimeter defenses, I think."

A likely story. And one Kat had heard before. After she'd come and introduced herself to Gray on Thursday, she'd inquired about his officers. She'd wanted to start with Rossiter and been told the same thing she was hearing now, and she had insisted on seeing the sergeant right away.

Lt. Henson had escorted her halfway across the compound to the border zone where the work crews were doing *their* job—but there'd been no sign of Rossiter, and no trail to follow. The man didn't even have his FURCS pad on him to be pinged.

Then she'd taken out her frustrations by rummaging around the guards' barracks and endearing herself to everyone. She'd started off on the wrong foot, but she'd managed to fix her relationship with the guards. However, her attempts to find out about Gray or Rossiter or anything else of import had been impeded at every turn.

"I don't think I'll bother traveling all that way to find out, *Colonel*." Kat seethed on the inside. "I'll take a look at your guards at the gate."

"That's important, sure." Gray nodded his approval. "Sgt. MacTierney can show you around." He buzzed his secretary and asked her to summon the sergeant. "How's your father doing? I suppose you speak to him regularly." To report, was the implication.

No, Kat did not. She hadn't seen her father for days, and that only in passing, but she didn't want to share that with this man, or anything else. At least she liked MacTierney. She liked the other sergeant and Lt. Henson as well. The only person here she hadn't cared for was Gray—unless she counted Rossiter, for whom she had gradually developed a deep loathing without even meeting the man. Prejudice plain and simple, but Kat couldn't help it.

"I don't want to disturb your digestion." Kat decided she needed to begin omitting any pretense of respect. Gray wasn't *her* boss—technically she was still assigned to Internal Security. "I'll just wait for MacTierney out there." And she turned and left for the lobby. She'd had enough of Gray for one day.

So much for the assignment Tony had saddled her with—Gray surely thought he was managing to handle Kat, and perhaps he was. She took a sharp look at the hard plastic seats in the outer office and decided to stand. She had hoped to needle Gray into revealing something, anything, of what he might be planning, but she couldn't abide being around the man for long enough.

She was supposed to investigate Rossiter, too, and she hadn't even been able to *find* him. The only thing Kat *had* succeeded at, as far as she could see, was becoming a decoy. And for that she hadn't had to *do* anything.

Ostensibly she was a liaison officer, a newly created post to help coordinate between Internal and External Security. Not that there was anything to coordinate. That had been the whole point.

As the daughter of the director, Kat was intended to be viewed as a plant. Everyone believed she'd be reporting back everything she saw and heard—she'd even made subtle jokes about that as part of her charm offensive.

The guards had been easy enough to win over. But if someone here was in league with Governor Roberts, they must not believe her sufficient threat. Not enough to try dealing with her in a more direct fashion. So much for being a target.

Tony had said her mere presence would suit his purposes. He'd surely expected Kat would proceed with her own investigation, though, knowing her as he did. That he'd not warned her off could be indulgence—but if he hoped she'd achieve anything extra, it looked as if he'd be sorely disappointed.

Kat was tired of waiting. Her lack of progress was creating a desire to take action and make something happen. She'd even begun patrolling alone at night, once she finished with the guards, as a way to try and deal with her impatience.

The outer door swung open, and Sgt. MacTierney marched in, giving Kat a smart salute. "At your service, mam."

She returned the salute even as she marveled at the diversity of reactions she'd garnered. Her rank as a security officer meant nothing here. The regular guards understood that she had no real authority over them, and they treated her like an officer—but in a casual, teasing manner.

The two sergeants she'd met, however, both behaved as if she were truly their superior, giving her due deference. Though nothing of the sort had been suggested as far as she was aware.

Lt. Henson, on the other hand, had treated her as a civilian—even making a pass at her.

Kat hadn't understood the differences in her reception, but she'd gone along with it, because it was important to her mission to let them feel comfortable around her. Though she wouldn't mind making Gray and Rossiter feel distinctly *un*comfortable.

She'd like to think those two were afraid of her, prompting Gray to try fobbing her off, and Rossiter to work hard avoiding her. But she suspected Chief Gray was actually enjoying the taunt. Playing keep away with the one person in whom she'd expressed an interest.

Kat sighed to herself and motioned MacTierney to precede her. "I want to see how things are done at the gate post." At least it was a short walk. Unlike the lengthy wild goose chase Gray had dangled in front of her. Checking the gate wouldn't take long, but this whole tangled assignment was of undetermined length. It could go on and on and on.

Three days in and Kat was beginning to suspect Tony had emphasized a real but tiny danger to lure her into accepting what in actuality would be nothing but prolonged tedium. Which was partly why she had started ignoring policy and patrolling at night—all on her own, like Tony.

Sgt. MacTierney looked over his shoulder and tried to talk as he walked. "It's been really exciting to have you here with us, Officer Miles. I mean a breath of fresh air, mam."

"Had it been boring before? With the possibility of an armed assault at any moment?" Kat knew she sounded sarcastic and tried again. "I'd expected to find everyone more on edge."

The sergeant blushed and turned back to watch his feet. "We were. At first."

"And then?"

"Three weeks and no excitement. Not here. I understand you—" The sergeant paused. He continued after clearing his throat. "Everything kind of relaxed some here, bit by bit."

Kat wondered what the guards were saying to each other about her, but she was more concerned about who might be spreading it, and even more she worried about this gradual relaxing of the guards. She tried to think how she could get more details out of the sergeant about how that was happening.

She was still considering what tack she might take when they arrived at the small square building set back from the main road. The natural light had completely gone by then, but the floodlights at the gate were glaring.

Kat stood and stared. The thick iron bars that spanned the gap in the wall seemed formidable, but the padlocked gate in the security fence didn't. She couldn't see much into the forest beyond, in spite of the lights.

She continued to examine the area as she asked, "Is no one at the actual gate?" She couldn't see any guards around. She turned to frown at her escort.

MacTierney looked distinctly uncomfortable, as well he should. "Well, since everything's sealed up, and without any visitors to check in or anything—"

"You do remember why we're on lockdown in the first place?"

"Yes, mam." The sergeant blushed. "But Colonel Gray said there was no use to having a man out there just to be target practice. Not when that's all there is to do, anyway."

She blinked. "There *is* something else a guard could do at the gate. He could *watch*."

Kat saw in MacTierney's eyes that he agreed. Nevertheless, he had a different answer ready for her. "There's a security camera on top of the fence, at that one corner," he said as he pointed at something lost in the glare of the lights.

So, Internal Security had no cameras anywhere, but the Guards had one conveniently pointed at the official approach to the compound. She wasn't sure which was more pathetic. "So who's 'watching'?" If that's what it could be called.

MacTierney coughed into this hand. "I'm not sure, but someone at HQ monitors the video feed."

Kat wondered who had been assigned that duty, if anyone. Perhaps that was the reason Sgt. Rossiter couldn't be found, but she still didn't like it. She was liking the whole setup less and less. It wouldn't take much for even a small force to get past the security fence, and the guards were clearly unprepared.

The perimeter wall was the best protection they had, but it wasn't really much of an improvement. The modifications Cameron's crew were busy making would help some, but not enough. Not against a military assault of the kind anticipated. Particularly not with an enemy in charge of the defense.

MacTierney cleared his throat again—his signal he wanted to speak and was asking for permission.

She wished he wouldn't do that. She'd rather not have to say, "Go ahead, Sergeant."

"Well, mam. I was just wondering what you're thinking." MacTierney blushed again. "The way you're staring at the gate."

Kat snorted. "I'm wondering why they haven't breached the fence already. It wouldn't take much and would make it easier for them when they attacked. But it would put us on the alert, and maybe they don't want that. Maybe they want us relaxed."

"Colonel Gray says—" The sergeant stumbled over his words as he met the look in her eye. "He says everyone's looking for a political solution."

"That may be, sergeant. But it's no excuse for a lack of vigilance. Because we don't know what they are actually *doing*." Which was true for her at least. *Is it true for Gray and Rossiter, too?* And she was beginning to have her doubts about how much Tony and her father knew.

"The colonel says they're waiting."

Kat agreed. In her opinion they *were* waiting, but likely not for a political solution, though who knew what a politician might define as a 'political' solution.

She realized she was tapping her toe against the ground and stopped. She gestured to the small hut-like structure. "The guards are in here, then?"

Sgt. MacTierney nodded and opened the door, preceding her into the tight quarters. At a small round table, two guards sat playing poker. Neither of them looked up from the game or acknowledged the sergeant's entrance, and it irked her. MacTierney introduced them as Mathers and Robinson.

Kat didn't try to hide her ire. "Only the two of you? I thought there were four guards on duty."

The two guards looked at each other for a long moment, but neither talked. So Kat turned back to MacTierney and cocked an eyebrow.

The sergeant frowned at the two men, but spoke to her. "I suppose the other two haven't returned from dinner."

"I don't recall seeing them in the mess." There had been only a few guards there, and Kat had taken the trouble to learn where they were headed when they finished.

"Colonel Gray started permitting the men to go out for meals if they wanted. Said it'd be good for morale. I could check where they've gone."

Kat shook her head. "Don't bother." Maybe she *was* discovering what she'd been searching for, because she believed she was starting to see a pattern emerge in Gray's incompetence, if such it could truly be considered. This relaxing of discipline was the key. *Not negligence, but design?*

This slack discipline wasn't consistent with the things she'd read in the man's file. Even if he preferred to delegate everything to avoid doing much work himself, he'd apparently always had a harsh hand on the whip to make sure his subordinates *did* stick to *their* duties. But *this*—Kat thought this looked like nothing so much as deliberate sabotage.

She grabbed MacTierney, turning her back on the pitiful excuses for guards, and pushed the sergeant ahead of her out the door. She knew he'd seen the same problems she'd discovered. However, he wasn't prepared to question his superiors and probably couldn't see the conclusions to which she was coming. That wasn't how soldiers were trained to think. But Kat was no soldier.

MacTierney had fallen behind her fast stride to trail after her. She slowed to allow him catch up and walk beside her.

"Mam?" At her nod, he continued. "What did you want to see next?"

Kat considered the question. She didn't intend to waste her time in a fruitless search for Sgt. Rossiter when the man could be anywhere and might well be actively avoiding her. But MacTierney had given her an idea.

"Sergeant, do you know where the feed from the security camera goes?"

"No, mam. I mean, not exactly."

She'd seen that the video didn't go to the guards in that tiny hut, which would have made the most sense. "You said headquarters, didn't you? I suppose you have a general idea where?"

Sgt. MacTierney wobbled his head. "I could just ask Colonel Gray where it is."

Kat shook her head. "Let's not bother the colonel. How about we just look around for ourselves. Maybe it'll turn up."

MacTierney looked ahead to the headquarters building as they approached the entrance. "I know where the feed isn't monitored. So maybe that gives me some inkling where it might be found."

"Good."

The guard on duty in the lobby saluted as they sailed through the entrance. And seeing him salute the sergeant helped to improve her mood—at least Gray's corrosive effect hadn't reached everywhere yet.

MacTierney silently led Kat down one corridor after another, until he stopped at the end of a hall with two doors on either side. He gestured at the door on the left. "That's a supply closet." He pointed at the other one. "I don't know what's in there, though."

She turned the knob as a matter of course. Of course it was locked—and it was the type that required a security key. She squinted at the door.

"Congratulations, Sergeant. I think you found what we were looking for."

She stood back as MacTierney stepped forward and knocked on the door. She watched him knock several times, waiting after each attempt, but there was no response.

The sergeant sighed. "I don't think anyone's in there. Must not be the right place."

MacTierney presumed someone would've been on duty. Kat did not. She took her keys from her pocket and considered. The security key Tony had given her was only supposed to work for their own offices. But she'd asked her new friend Ben to do a particular favor for her—only she didn't know if he had managed it yet. At least there was an easy way to find out.

She plugged the security key into her FURCS pad and pressed her thumb against the pad as she inserted the key and turned. The lock disengaged and she opened the door while the sergeant looked on with awe.

Kat elected not to disillusion the man. If he believed she had more authority than she really had, it might come in handy in the future. She just grinned wide.

They both stuck their heads inside before entering the room, which was small and unoccupied. It contained only an empty chair and a large screen set into the wall—a screen displaying live video of the road as it approached the main gate. MacTierney looked thoroughly around the room before turning to her and swallowing hard. "Um..."

The sergeant was upset and starting to sweat—maybe this was too much adventure for him.

Kat took another quick look around the room and nodded to herself. "Let's leave before someone shows up."

MacTierney looked relieved as he followed her out. "Where to now, mam?"

"The firing range." Kat liked to shoot while she did her deep thinking. "I'd like to get off a few practice rounds." And some steam while she was at it. She glanced over her shoulder at the sergeant. "By the way. Everything you just saw, what we did, forget it. Don't. Tell. Anyone."

The man just nodded his head, but his smile implied that he would obey her instructions. After he watched her shoot, there wouldn't be any doubt.

She remembered how Tony had taken her to the firing range to give her a lesson as a gift for her fifteenth birthday, and he'd continued teaching her how to shoot. But she had room for improvement. Maybe later she could get lessons from Ken Cameron, since he was an expert.

Right now, Kat wanted to obliterate some helpless paper targets. Then she'd leave this place and head out for her solo patrol—if Tony could ignore policy, so could she.

Chapter 11

Home is Where

7:05 p.m. Monday, December 16th

DAVID lay on top of his bed staring at the ceiling, once again trying to organize the puzzle pieces floating around in his head, attempting to fit them into a picture that made sense. He no longer trusted his own judgment. He wished he could talk through his problem with another person to get a different take on the dilemma he struggled with, but several obstacles stood in the way.

He was no longer sure who he could trust without qualification. Still lacking proof of anything, he wondered who'd listen to him long enough to fully discuss the implications. Even when all put together, the things he'd seen amounted to only a sketch—a rude outline, nothing real or tangible. He needed some tiny sliver of concrete evidence.

Though he wasn't sure he actually wanted that evidence, tonight he would try again to acquire it. Because somehow his mother was mixed up in everything. Until David knew the what and the how of his mom's involvement, he wouldn't be able to move on to anything else. Nevertheless, he feared what he might learn.

He remembered waking in up in this same bed on Saturday morning, dazed and disoriented, with the morning sun glaring into his room. Then the bright daylight had sent an alarm buzzing through his brain that he was late for work. Though he'd still been lying across the bed when his boss had barged into the room.

Ken hadn't looked angry, only concerned. David's mother had already sent his boss the message that her son wasn't feeling well, though it was nothing serious, and he wouldn't be showing up to work. Still Ken had come to see for himself.

David had been touched. And while half asleep, he'd tried to tell his boss about his discoveries. He didn't remember what he'd said, but it must've been fairly incoherent—since Ken had barked something about how he should stop spouting nonsense. His boss had suggested David was suffering heatstroke, or possibly dehydration, or maybe plain over work.

Ken had told David to take care and not worry about coming back to work until he was ready, and then left without listening to another word. Which frustrated David, who really needed to talk to someone. He had hoped to discuss the situation with his boss, who was one person David felt sure he could trust. And he respected Ken's opinions.

After that he must have drifted in and out, because the next thing he could remember was jerking awake at the sound of Crystal entering the house on Saturday afternoon. Returning from her other job—and that thought had jolted him to sudden clarity.

He'd hopped into the shower to reinvigorate his mind and body, so he could bring all his faculties to bear on his problem. After assuring Crystal he was fine so she wouldn't interrupt his cogitation, David had sat at his desk and tried to recapture the ideas that had floated through his brain the night before. For all they might have been the delusions of sleep deprivation.

Then as now he'd taken each element and tested it and tried to see the different ways it might fit with the others. He hadn't found the solution, but he had decided on a plan of action.

He'd done his best to act normal when his mom had come home from work and when they'd all sat down to dinner. He'd assured his mother and Crystal that he was feeling much improved. The way he had scarfed down a giant plate of pasta had likely been more convincing than his words.

His mom had retired to her study to finish up some work, and Crystal had gone back to the dorm to spend the rest of the weekend catching up with some friends. Or so she'd said. Either way it had helped clear the field for David. He'd waited in his room, lying wide awake on his bed, just as he did now, in preparation for the same task. Perhaps this time he would succeed.

After him mom had retired for the night, David had waited over an hour to make as sure as he could that she'd have fallen asleep. Then he'd crept out of his room in the dark and headed down to her study. He had moved slow and managed to avoid breaking his neck on the stairs, then succeeded in banging into various pieces of furniture, causing himself a fair amount of pain but little noise.

As he'd expected, his mother had left her work-pad sitting on her desk. In the dark with the door closed, and Crystal hopefully gone in truth, he had tried to guess the password. His attempts with his birthday, his mom's, both of their middle names—all had failed. He'd even tried his father's name, but that hadn't worked either.

He had given up for the night, more in anxiety than frustration, because he didn't know how many failed attempts it would take to trigger something.

David tried to tell himself that he hadn't done anything that would alert his mother to the intrusion. Clearly he didn't make much of a hacker.

Then he'd been thwarted again when his mom had taken her workpad to the office early on Sunday morning before services, and left it there. Hoping she'd bring it home the following evening, he had wracked his brains in the meantime.

He'd decided this was his best opportunity for finding the evidence which would either indict or exculpate his mother, and he wasn't about to throw in the towel. He had searched her study earlier this morning, while his mom and Crystal were away, in case she'd written her password down somewhere. With plenty of time and light, he had looked around thoroughly. But he'd found nothing.

Tonight, David planned to try again to get into his mother's files. As usual, she hadn't come home for dinner. So he'd eaten with Crystal, and after she had cleaned up and retired for the night, he'd gone to his room to wait.

He didn't know what time it was when he heard the front door and knew his mom had returned, and he didn't bother to check his wrist. He just went to stand at the top of the stairs and look down into the foyer. He didn't see her then, but several minutes later she came climbing up the stairs, and she gave her son a weary smile when she noticed him.

David smiled back, stepping aside as his mother reached the landing. "Welcome home."

"It's nice to be home." She sighed, shrugging off her jacket and massaging her shoulder. "Did you have a nice dinner?"

David grinned. "Better than yours I expect."

"Mine was fine." His mom continued down the hallway. "But it's difficult to enjoy your food when you're working."

"I could fix hot chocolate. To help you unwind."

"Thanks, but I'm just going to shower and relax for a bit before finishing up some work." And saying that, she went into the master bedroom at the end of the hall.

David took a long, deep breath. He waited another minute to be sure, then quietly descended the steps and made straight for his mom's study. She hadn't brought her workpad upstairs with her, so he expected she'd left it in the study as usual. He found it there on top of the desk.

The lights were all on, and he didn't know how much time he had, so he sat right down and turned on the pad. He was trying to remember what passwords he'd decided to try, and in what order, when he realized with a shock that the pad was unlocked.

His mother must've logged on briefly when she came home and forgotten to log out. She'd looked *that* tired. Remembering that he hadn't much time to waste, David stopped dawdling and searched the recent activity logs.

It required several minutes for him to decipher the various files and find what he wanted. He took out his own FURCS pad, because he didn't want to leave any more traces than he might have already, and snapped a picture of the screen. The one showing what his mom had been doing with her access codes, with time and date stamps. The incriminating evidence.

David sat there stunned for several minutes as he tried to process the information. He could only imagine one explanation. His own mother had been conspiring with Governor Roberts.

Though he'd been unable to find any details of their plot in the files, the fact of their collusion appeared to be inescapable. He could only guess at the specifics, but he no longer cared about them.

He carefully set the pad back on the desk as he'd found it—and wondered whether he should leave it unlocked, or log out and hope his mother wouldn't realize she'd forgotten to do that herself. He chose to log off the workpad.

He left the study and went to stand in the foyer, staring up the staircase and thinking that his mother would be down soon. He'd found the evidence he'd been seeking. Now he wasn't sure what he should do with it—except he knew he didn't want to stay here while he considered. David certainly wasn't ready to face his mom, so he opened the front door and left the house.

The night sky was heavy with clouds pressing down on the lights dotting the neighborhood. He breathed in the fresh, moist air with its promise of incipient rain. David almost turned back to grab his umbrella, but found himself reluctant to enter the house again.

He rubbed the underside of his wrist and saw it was barely a quarter 'til eight. He'd think while he walked. He ambled away aimlessly, allowing his mind and feet both to wander where they willed.

He realized he would have to do *something* with the information he'd just found. But this was his own mother. Before he took any irrevocable action, he wanted to be sure he was doing the right thing.

Three times he'd tried to tell his boss about his suspicions, but Ken hadn't wanted to listen—and if David *could* get his attention with what he had now, he knew what would happen. His boss would insist on taking the evidence to the proper authorities and leaving it with them. Whatever the consequences of that might be.

David hoped to find a way to solve his problem, to deal with the plot without exposing his mom. But that would require a more nuanced approach. Perhaps it was foolish, but he'd have to try.

David tried to think of what person in a position of authority he could trust most to help him. Not his mother, under the circumstances.

Director Miles was above suspicion, but even if David dared to speak to the man, whom he'd never met in all the years his mom had worked for him, that would be no help. It would only put his mother in the worst possible position.

He looked around the empty street as he walked on. His feet had taken him by habit down the sidewalk along the main road, toward the gate where he had often waited for Ken in the morning. Close to the Guard Headquarters.

Lt. Henson had certainly been willing to listen. And the lieutenant had shared his own doubts about Chief Gray, so it seemed unlikely he was a part of the conspiracy himself.

He wouldn't have encouraged David's questions and amateur investigation if the man had anything to hide. And Henson had the authority to act. Since the man hadn't been willing to do anything when it was all speculation, perhaps he'd show similar caution now there was evidence.

Altogether, it caused David to hope for the more nuanced approach he sought—and he did need to share with someone. He thought Lt. Henson was his best choice. He could try talking to the man at least, and see if it felt right before committing himself.

Thus decided, David crossed the empty street, heading through the dark to the Guard HQ. It started raining just as the door was closing behind him.

He went right up to the guard in the lobby. "Is Lt. Henson in?"

The man nodded slightly and hit a button on his FURCS pad. "The Belue kid is here. Wants to see you." After a pause, he waved David down the hallway.

The lieutenant stood just inside his office, holding the door open with an easy smile—which would probably fade when he heard what David brought.

Henson shut the door and crossed to sit behind his desk. "Since it's a little late for a visit, I'm assuming this is something important."

"Very." David looked around the office and put his hand on the back of a chair.

The lieutenant eased back in his own chair and gestured to David. "Please, take your time."

David found himself staring at the chair in front of him for a long moment before shaking his head.

Henson's countenance turned serious. "Is this about Gray or Rossiter, or maybe that Crystal person?"

David took a deep breath, his hands clenching the padding on the back of the chair. "You're still concerned?" David paused as he tried to order his thoughts. "I guess it's about all three."

"All three?" The lieutenant scratched his nose. "Well, I'm pretty sure Colonel Gray has been sabotaging things here, but in small ways. Hard to do anything about, because it's not even obvious negligence." Henson nodded to himself. "I think he's unlikely to do too much damage, though. Do you have anything more on Rossiter?"

"I told you about his visits to the Rec Center and the vanishing duffel bag. Definitely something fishy there."

"Without a doubt." The lieutenant seemed to chew it over for a minute. "I've looked into it, but so far I haven't found any evidence." His face turned grim. "Probably smuggling contraband. Black market stuff. How bad that could be—depends on what it is he's got in the bag."

David returned the grim look. "I've still no idea what's in the bag, or to whom he's delivering it, but I don't think it's that simple. Because he's definitely doing something that ties back to the governor."

"You're sure?"

David eased his hands off the back of the chair and forced himself to sit down in it. "I told you of the sergeant's night visit to my house. I thought he was there to meet Crystal."

"This housekeeper of yours that you suspect?"

David sighed. "I don't know about Crystal anymore. But what I do believe is that Rossiter went to the house to meet my mother. And that it's all to do with Governor Roberts."

"Hold on, David." Henson leaned forward. "I'm not following. Your mother?"

David fidgeted in the chair. "I don't want to get her in trouble."

"I have a duty, a responsibility." The lieutenant looked David straight in the eye. "There are different ways to discharge one's duties, though." Henson seemed to search around for something more to say. "I'll take your concerns into consideration, but I'm afraid I can't promise more than that."

David nodded. "I understand." It would have to be good enough. His choices were limited.

The lieutenant waited while David took his time trying to decide exactly what to say.

David stared at the top of the desk and cleared his throat. "I couldn't find anything to back up my suspicions of Crystal. I couldn't help but start wondering about my mom—whether she'd been the one meeting Rossiter." He didn't see the need to drag in Caroline Sanderson. "My own mother. I had to find out one way or the other."

"Sure. I get that."

"I got a look at the files on her workpad. She takes it home in the evening." Now he was committing himself. "I examined her recent activity logs, and there's no question. She's been using her access codes—the ones that let her change the restrictions on the FURCS communication node. She's been in contact with Governor Roberts. Multiple times."

Henson's voice was soft. "Still, it could be something legitimate. Negotiations?"

David shook his head without looking up. "That doesn't explain Sgt. Rossiter's visit." He didn't want to hear the excuses he'd tried to tell himself. "And I checked the time and date stamps of those communications." He felt himself deflate in the chair. "She contacted the governor while Rossiter was there, in the house. That's no coincidence."

The lieutenant frowned. "No, I can see there's only one conclusion to draw."

"I think she's involved in something shady with Governor Roberts. Giving him the ability to communicate with conspirators inside the compound. That would make her one of them." David thought she could well be in charge of the whole plot, whatever that might be, but he wouldn't mention that. He was trying to get his mother out of trouble, not into more.

"You're not in the mood to hear this." Henson offered a weak smile. "But your deductions, your results—they're pretty impressive. I have to admit I didn't expect so much."

David sighed. He didn't want to hear that. "But the question remains—what now?"

The lieutenant breathed in and out and worked his jaw for several moments before he responded. "Technically, this is a matter for Internal Security. They have a liaison officer here, but I believe she's already left for the day." Henson paused to rub his earlobe. "I *should* take this straight to Chief Nelson or Director Miles. But let's table that for the moment and see if we have any alternatives."

"I appreciate it." David sat up in his chair. "But if this is an urgent problem, I don't want to be responsible for delaying any action." He wondered if they could find another way.

"I don't know that it's urgent. Serious, yes."

David hated to shake his head. "If my mom is facilitating messages being passed between Roberts and Gray—" He'd given this a lot of thought and was satisfied to see the lieutenant paying full attention. "They could use that communication to coordinate sabotage by Gray on the inside with an attack from the outside." That's why David had been compelled to say something to someone. "The results could be devastating."

Henson sat back in his chair and scratched his nose while he thought. "Your mother. She can't—won't want to be seen acting in the open. Same goes for Gray. They have to keep everything secret." The lieutenant paused for another long moment. "That's their disadvantage."

David thought he saw where Lt. Henson's mind was headed, a benefit of his having stewed over the problem so much. "We have our own disadvantage, though. We don't know exactly what it is they might be planning. Worse, we don't know how close they may be to implementing whatever it is."

"True. But I'm not sure we need to know." Henson sat forward again and looked David in the eye. "Not in order to use *their* disadvantage to create an opportunity. All we have to do is keep any messages from being passed in the meantime."

David shook his head. "How can we do that? We know Sgt. Rossiter must've been relaying things between my mother and Gray, and presumably the governor. I still suspect Crystal. For all we know there could be others."

The lieutenant smiled. "But as long as we can contain any communication with the people on the outside, we can delay whatever they're planning. It buys us time."

David leaned forward onto the edge of his seat. "But how? And what do we do with the time, if we can get it?"

Henson frowned. "Let's look at the opportunity first. The director himself sent his daughter here as a so-called liaison officer—the motive is transparent. The administration's already unhappy with the job Gray's doing. Her report won't help Gray. They will just use it as a lever to get rid of the man. I can do my part by putting in my own report, revealing some of the problems I've seen with Colonel Gray. And once they've replaced him..."

"Then the threat he poses is neutralized." David wondered if part of Henson's plan was designed to get himself promoted, but he didn't care. "The danger Gray poses flows from his authority. If *that* is taken away, it certainly hobbles what the conspirators could do." It was a promising idea, but it left some loose ends. A threat would remain. "There's still Rossiter." *And my mother.*

"I know all about the sergeant. And the director's daughter clearly has her suspicions. Without Gray around, I doubt that Rossiter would be able to pull anything."

David returned to the more immediate issue. "So how do we keep my mother from coordinating anything until Gray's gone?"

"No offense, but I don't believe we can rely on your surveillance. Not when it's this serious." The lieutenant paused in thought. "I'll have to make up something to get Rossiter out the way for a while. I have a couple of guards I can trust, who can be discreet." Henson ran his thumbnail up and down the bridge of his nose. "They can watch your mom."

David agreed that his own efforts would be lacking, but he was unsure of the rest. "Can you find a way to deal with the sergeant? And will two men be enough to keep an eye on my mother?"

"Yes. She won't be able to make a move when she's at work, so they'd only have to keep her under surveillance outside of that. And she can't communicate with them over the FURCSnet—there'd be too much chance of getting caught. So it's feasible. And I can keep an eye on Gray personally."

David nodded. It seemed like it might work, but it was a big chance to take. They only needed it to work for a short time, though. "If this works, then I wouldn't have to worry about my mother being exposed?"

"Not from me."

"I want to do my part. I can watch Crystal, just in case."

Henson grinned. "You do that. And I'll get the ball rolling on my end right away, by taking care of Sgt. Rossiter."

David stood, offering the lieutenant his hand. He felt relieved. He'd shared his burden, unloaded onto someone with authority who could and would do something about it, and in a way that might keep his mother out of it completely. After they shook hands, Henson rose and walked with David out and down the corridor before turning back.

David's steps were lighter as he crossed the lobby and waved to the guard. He walked right out into the rain. He stood outside in the dark and let the rain fall and didn't mind that he was getting soaked. It felt good.

He started strolling up the sidewalk without giving a thought to where he was going or why. He'd told the lieutenant he'd keep an eye on Crystal, but he doubted that was necessary. He should head to the house anyway. It would take Henson a while to make his arrangements, and David could watch his mother in the interim. But he couldn't make himself do that.

He was weary with the effort of the past weeks, and despite sleeping most of the weekend away he still felt like crashing. He still had his dorm room, and he let his feet meander in that direction. He was beginning to get water-logged now.

As his soggy clothes grew heavy, his thoughts grew heavy as well. He hadn't been forthright with Lt. Henson, for all he'd wanted to share. He hadn't told the man about Caroline Sanderson's activities, or how he suspected his own mother's involvement to be deeper than he'd intimated. And even if they *could* manage to thwart Chief Gray, the community remained under serious threat. And any number of potential enemies would remain on the loose— capable of doing unknown harm.

The full impact of David's choice began to dawn upon him. He had put his concern for his mom, for protecting her, above everyone else's safety. Ahead of everything. He loved his mother. But he should have just gone straight to Director Miles with what he'd found, all of it. That's what Ken would've told him to do.

Now David could only hope that this alternate solution he'd grabbed at to make things easier for himself—that it didn't backfire and create a terrible mess for them all. *What if it's not enough, or not in time?* As right as it had seemed at the time, now he was having second thoughts.

The pouring rain no longer refreshed him as it streamed down his face. Up ahead he saw the Green with its already dim lights almost completely extinguished by the downpour. He was well past the side street leading to his own house. And the dorms felt far too distant to him now. He glimpsed one of the wooden benches that sat, dotting around the sidewalk that circled the Green, and managed to make it that far, his feet dragging.

He sat down with a muffled thump and squish. He propped his elbows on his knees and his face in his hands and just let the wall of water wash over him. He drifted. He didn't know how long he sat there, quietly drowning in the dark, before he realized he needed to ask for help.

David started praying. *Lord, if you can hear, I no longer know what to do. I want to do what's*

right, but I can't seem to understand anything any-
more. It's too much for me. I can't handle it. God,
help me. God help us all.

David continued to sit in the pouring rain, helpless and wondering how he'd managed to get to this
point. He'd started by trying to do what he thought
was right. But somewhere along the way he'd gotten
off track. Somehow he'd lost his direction. And he
no longer had the energy to do anything about it.

Then he heard the sharp voice over the sound of
the falling rain.

"You look like a drowned rat. I should lock you
up for your own good. At least it would keep you
warm and dry."

Chapter 12

When it Pours

8:50 p.m. Monday, December 16th

KAT looked down at the sad, pathetic figure on the bench as he lifted his head at the sound of her voice. She saw his hair was plastered with rain, and water was streaming down his face like a river, and while she must have looked a picture herself, it couldn't be as bad as this poor trout. She hoped.

She couldn't tell if the kid had been crying, but he looked about as low as anyone she'd ever seen. He just sat there, staring at her. She couldn't allow him to stay here and catch his death of cold. "There aren't any proper cells at Security. Hopefully no one will mind if I park you in the break room while you dry off. And get some hot food in you."

"Security?" The boy lifted his head a little now and looked at her.

"Yes, I'm a security officer, though you wouldn't know it." And Kat wondered why she was wasting her time babbling to this stranger.

"You. I know who you are."

Kat sighed because she knew where this was going, and she'd grown tired of it. The kid gazed at her with widening eyes. *He might be a bit dim.*

With the dark and the roar of the rain, Kat didn't sense anything until a tiny tingle of a presence just behind her gave too little warning, and then she was being pushed roughly aside, shoved to the ground. As she rolled and spun around on the wet grass, she saw the form of her attacker as he went straight for the boy on the bench, going in low with a knife.

Kat rolled right back up to him without pausing and sprung to her feet with one arm thrusting up under the man's right elbow, punching her palm into the bottom his chin. She started to shift behind him for a throw, but he was already turning into her, sinking his weight as he jammed his elbow into her shoulder and pushing her back.

Kat started to lose her balance, slipping as the knife flashed up and out toward her face. She let herself drop back, grabbing his sleeve and using her falling weight to pull him with her, closer in, as his knife hand stretched past where her head had been.

Then she shifted back in as he fell into her, folding his arm in on itself and driving the knife home.

Her attacker's eyes flew open wide. His mouth gaped, and he coughed up a bit of blood with a soft moan before jerking in her arms, just for a moment. Then he collapsed.

Kat eased his body to the ground, with the rain already washing away the small amount of blood. She had never killed before but knew she had now. She wondered who he had been and why he'd been trying to kill the kid.

She turned to look at that boy. Dazed and white enough to shine in the darkness, he struggled to his feet. He took a tentative step forward, looking down at the body. "Rossiter."

Rossiter? Kat worked hard not to gape herself. It seemed she had found her wayward sergeant, and her investigation of the man was over before it had begun. That didn't tell her what his connection was with this kid. She had plenty of questions to ask, but this wasn't the time or place for an interrogation.

Kat looked around at the empty night. Quiet except for the constant drumming of the downpour, and no one in sight. She could leave the body here for now. She needed to get to the office to tell Tony what had happened and to get herself and the boy out of the rain so they could dry off. Then she'd find out what in the deep blue sea this was about.

Kat couldn't keep thinking of him of as 'kid' so she asked, "What's your name?"

He looked from the body on the ground back to her. "David. David Belue."

So. She knew who he must be. She still hadn't been able to read Verity's file, but this would be the woman's son. Even without getting the details from him, the whole thing already made a kind of sense to her, though she wasn't sure why. She reached out to grab his elbow. She wouldn't be releasing this catch until she'd landed him safe into Security Headquarters.

The boy didn't resist when she pulled him away from the scene, and she had no trouble guiding him along the sidewalk circling the Green. The kid was finding his feet well enough, but she didn't want to hurry him. He'd come close enough to a poor end tonight. Kat didn't want to risk letting him trip and split his head on the concrete.

Her right hand piloted the boy forward, and her left massaged her shoulder while she thanked God that Rossiter hadn't had the leverage to make that blow as hard as it could've been. Her shoulder was aching plenty as it was.

She needed to get out of this wet night and into some dry clothes and a warm bed, and grab herself serious shut-eye. She'd have to wait a while though, for the change and for the sleep.

Even moving slow, Kat maneuvered her charge back to the office in no time, dragging him through the door to be greeted by the sight of Hope's bright smile. Tony had adopted the scheme Kat had suggested. Hope was now a safety aide, not an officer trainee, and much happier to sit behind a desk instead of going out on patrol.

Kat smiled back. "Please tell me the boss is in?"

Hope nodded and buzzed them through. Then she came around to help keep the kid from slipping on the slick floor, onto which they were both dripping mightily. And if the girl had any curiosity, she didn't ask any questions. She simply sat back down at the duty desk and gestured at Tony's office.

Out of the darkness and into the lighted building, the boy seemed less confused—so Kat pinched him on the arm just to check. He turned his head and gave her a sharp look. Then he nodded.

Kat needed to do more, if she was going to get him in shape to be helpful. She pushed him down the hall until she got him into the break room and onto one of the hard plastic chairs. Where the water dripping off him started to pool.

One thing at a time. She poured the last dregs of coffee into a guest mug and began brewing another pot. She cringed at the strong stale crude that half-filled the mug, then shrugged. The kid could surely use the jolt.

Kat set it down on the table in front of him and waited to see if he would pick it up on his own. He reached out slowly, grabbed it and brought it close, peering into its depths.

Then he turned to look at her. "Honey."

Kat started. Then she saw him return his stare to the coffee, and it clicked. She had no use for the stuff herself, but she knew where it was kept and got a bottle from the bottom cupboard. She handed it over and watched him turn it upside down over the mug and squeeze. And keep pouring honey into his coffee until the mug was full. Well, the kid could use the sugar right now, and it wouldn't hurt the sludge any, but it almost made her nauseous to watch.

She couldn't stand around taking care of him, though. She needed to catch Tony before he disappeared on her, but she couldn't leave the boy here alone. So she popped down the hall to find Susan doing reports in the conference room.

"Susan, I need a hand for a moment."

Kat darted back down the hall at Susan's nod. The woman followed her with quick strides back to the break room. The kid was still sitting there in a small pond and focusing on getting the sludge from the mug down his throat.

Kat turned back to Susan with a pleading look. "Sorry for this, but someone needs to keep an eye on him while I have a quick word with the boss." Taking Susan's acceptance for granted, Kat dived back down the corridor to Tony's office. She breezed in without knocking, closing the door behind her.

She stood before his desk, dripping quietly onto the carpet while Tony looked up and stared at her a long moment. Then he leaned back in his chair and grinned like a baboon.

Kat had been in too much of a rush to consider her appearance, and she wondered what she must look like, but she didn't dare check in the mirror to see. Well, she'd always taken care to dress professional for this job before. She knew she'd appeared sharp enough when she gave him the interim report just this morning. *He'd best remember that.*

She stepped over to one of the filing cabinets and grabbed herself a towel from the top drawer. She talked as she scrubbed her hair dry. "I found Rossiter." Then she remembered about the boy and snatched a second towel to take back with her.

"And?"

Kat fluffed her hair back out as best she could with her hand. "You can find what's left of the sergeant over by the Green. He was trying to kill this kid."

Tony wasn't grinning any longer. "Kill a kid?" He'd leaned forward to listen to her.

"I've got him parked in the break room for now, but I need to get back and dry him off."

Tony looked irritable. "Who is he, and what's going on, and are you seriously telling me you left a dead body on the Green?"

Kat tossed the used towel over the back of a chair. "David Belue. You'll want to hear his story." So would Kat. If Tony thought she'd already heard, then maybe he'd let her stick around and listen.

"How about you?" Tony sounded miffed. "Can you tell me *your* story, or do you need to go change clothes first?"

It would be nice, she thought, but there was too much that needed doing in a hurry. "I'm good. And yes, there's a corpse on the Green." She was gratified to have Tony's full and complete attention.

Kat pursed her lips as she weighed exactly what she would say next. She probably shouldn't explain about patrolling alone at night—even if Tony were already aware of what she was doing, it would best be left unstated.

"I found the kid sitting on one of the benches. I don't think Rossiter even knew who I was—he just went straight for the boy with a knife. I did what I had to do. The sergeant is dead, and I brought the kid back here." *End of story.*

Tony opened his mouth a few times, but bit off whatever he'd considered saying, which she thought wise of him. In the end, he stood and walked to his office's back door. "Where exactly is the body?"

Kat told him and watched him go, then she took another of Tony's towels. She took them back to the break room, where she found David more alert and gulping down a mug of freshly brewed coffee, with plenty of honey no doubt.

Susan must've been busy cleaning. Because the floor was dry for the moment, and the kid no longer sat in the middle of a lake. Now she was rummaging through the cupboards.

Susan pulled down a plastic-wrapped package and waved it at Kat. "I'm trying to find something to just zap, to get hot food for the poor kid. It's either popcorn or some of those frozen frog legs."

Kat blinked. None of her colleagues should be deprived of their popcorn. "He needs protein."

Susan shrugged and replaced the popcorn and turned to the fridge. "I'll get it going, but then I need to get back to my own job."

Kat nodded and watched as Susan suited action to words and then left. While she waited on the frog legs, Kat handed David the pair of towels—pleased to see him get right to work drying himself off more. And his color was coming back.

She refrained from saying anything until he had started to eat. "My boss—" Which wouldn't mean anything to this kid. "Chief of Internal Security Anthony Nelson. He'll want to hear what you have to say for yourself. But he won't be back for a bit."

Because he's busy disposing of a dead body. Kat didn't feel the need to share that with the kid, who was still an unknown quantity to her. She suspected Tony knew more that *he* wasn't sharing. But maybe if she listened closely she would pick up some clues when he questioned David.

She looked at the boy, who now had half a frog leg hanging out of his mouth. "So consider how you can explain things. But save your story for my boss."

He looked up at her as the frog leg disappeared. "I don't need to consider anything."

"I said save it. Can't you listen?" Kat heard herself snap, and it reminded her that this kid wasn't the only one in need of repair. She tossed in one of the microwave popcorn bags, and while it popped, she went back to massaging her shoulder.

Kat wished she'd taken Tony up on his offer to go change clothes, because they were feeling quite waterlogged now, but it would have to wait a little longer. But she could pour herself a mug of freshly brewed coffee, and she did. *Black.*

She sat down across the table from David with her coffee and her popcorn. It felt good to get off her feet for a moment. She sipped coffee and munched popcorn while she considered the boy.

While Tony had ended up sharing Chief Gray's file, he'd continued to refuse to let her see the Belue woman's. The woman who had been working as her father's right hand for a number of years now. Kat wondered if that was Tony's own stubbornness or her father's at work, and rued that she'd never paid much attention to the glorified secretary.

She'd not even known the woman had a son. *Or I would've looked up his file.* Then she'd know more about him, assuming Tony hadn't removed that file as well.

Those qualified to attend FedU, as the students called it, were supposedly pretty bright, though she hadn't seen evidence of that in David. Kat had seen too much stupid behavior from those very same students to give much credit to their screening process. She thought it likely strings had been pulled.

Then she saw Tony poke his head around the corner and wink at her. She downed the rest of her coffee and stood, reaching over to grab the kid with one hand while she kept the bag of popcorn in the other. She took them both down the hall to Tony's office, ready to be entertained.

She sat David down in one of the chairs facing Tony's desk and whipped the wet towel away, throwing it onto the other chair—then she stood off to one side, leaning on a filing cabinet and munching her popcorn.

Tony glared at her for a moment. Then he focused in sharply on the boy. "You're David Belue? Verity's son?"

"Yes, sir."

Tony took a long moment before asking another question. "How do you know Sgt. Rossiter?"

The boy nodded in approval. "From the beginning."

David sat up straight in the chair and stared into the distance. "Rossiter was in charge of supervising the guard detail assigned to protect my work crew in the buffer zone. But the man barely spent any time there, and when he was around, he was always fiddling with what I assumed was his FURCS pad. Now I think it might have been a regular cell phone. It seemed off to me, and when I realized that he might be trying to find where he could get a signal from an outside cell tower I became suspicious."

The kid described how he'd decided to try and follow the sergeant. How that led to his finding out about Chief Gray, at least enough to feed his suspicions, and how neither his boss nor his mother nor Lt. Henson had seemed inclined to do much without more evidence. Which was why he had decided to start his own investigation.

David detailed what he'd seen following the sergeant and what he'd guessed from that. How seeing Rossiter's surreptitious exit from his own house had led him to investigate their part-time housekeeper Crystal, and how that had eventually led him to discover Caroline Sanderson's skullduggery.

Kat fought the urge to laugh as she listened to his description of her mother's performance. She paused with a handful of popcorn halfway to her mouth, afraid of chocking as she pictured Caroline behaving like a spy in a cheap thriller. Which would be par for the course, really.

She lost her sense of humor, though, when she heard what the boy had found on his mother's work-pad. And when he told how he'd hoped to keep her from being exposed. She thought David was coming clean with them, but Tony would evaluate his story better that she. What irked Kat was this untrained kid, acting on his own hook, had hauled in a bigger catch than her own investigation.

At the end of the recitation, Tony stood up and loomed over the boy. "I'm glad you're finally telling me all this. It would've been better, though, if you'd shared your suspicions with me from the start and stayed out of it yourself. You almost got killed. You almost got Officer Miles killed, even if she doesn't realize it. And the Lord only knows what other con-sequences your actions may have had." Tony gave up the glaring. "I know you're tired, David, but I'm going to take you through everything again, in more detail."

Tony glanced at Kat with a twinkle in his eye. "But first, I need to have a word with this young la-dy."

Tony walked around his desk and brought Kat over to the office door. He spoke quickly, keeping his voice low. "We need to understand exactly why Rossiter wanted to kill David, and particularly why now. Something precipitated that move. Maybe I'll have a better grasp of the possibilities once I've gone through it with him one more time."

Kat was too tired think, at least for now, but she would have to try to work it out later. "Alright, what do you want me to do?"

"I want you to go home." Tony was holding her by her still soaked shirt. "Get into some dry clothes and get some rest."

"Okay." She didn't want to argue. Besides, she wasn't interested in listening to the boy re-tell his story. She wanted to hear Tony's thoughts about all this. But she couldn't force him to share.

"I'll find someone else to escort the boy over to his dorm room, once I've finished with him." Tony opened the door for her. "And tomorrow I'll talk to you about what's going on, what you need to know."

Kat nodded and slipped out the door. She did need the rest, and now she'd be looking forward to getting some more information out of her boss. But she didn't want that exchange to be one-sided. And as she was going home, she could use the opportunity of 'bonding' to drag something out of her mother. And bring that to the table, for Tony.

As Kat was headed out the door into the rain, Hope reached out and took the popcorn bag out of her hand and replaced it with an umbrella. *A nice thought, Hope, but too late.* Still Kat snapped open the thing as she stepped out into the night.

She could've gone one better and driven one of the carts home and saved her weary legs in addition to arriving faster. But by the time it had occurred to her, she was already trudging past the Green. She couldn't help but glance at the spot where Rossiter's body had lain, though it was hard to see it now.

Part of her training had been preparation for a situation where one had to take a life, but the possibility had always seemed so remote. Now Kat *had* killed someone, but she was too tired to remember how she was supposed to deal with that. She would wait for Tony's inevitable lecture to remind her.

When she got home, she let herself in the front door and dropped the umbrella in the hall and went looking for Caroline. Only half past ten and surely the woman would be awake, somewhere. Kat didn't have a clue where, though, and it took ten minutes before she found her mother in her father's study.

She'd poked her head in to see Caroline curled up in one of the big leather chairs. With a book and a cup of cocoa. She walked in and considered what approach to take, waiting for her mother to notice her presence.

Caroline raised her head from her book and immediately set her things down and hurried over to grab Kat's shirt in both hands. She rubbed the wet fabric and frowned. "Darling, you must get out of these clothes right away."

Kat frowned back. "I'd rather intended to, after I've got a pot of coffee brewing." She removed her mother's hands and started to turn.

Caroline reached out to snag Kat's arm. "What you need is a nice mug of hot chocolate. You've had too much coffee already, I expect." She pushed her daughter out the door and down the hall. Not to the kitchen where Kat wanted to go, but all the way to the bottom of the stairs.

"Mother—"

"Hush. I'll make it for you and bring it up. You hurry up and change—into that fuzzy robe I gave you for your birthday. Then you can relax."

Kat sighed. But she decided she'd best humor Caroline, since she hoped to put her enough at ease to discover something. She'd consider how to accomplish that after getting comfortable.

She felt her mother's eyes on her back until she was halfway up the stairs, then heard Caroline walk off in the direction of the kitchen, to make some hot chocolate for her daughter. Kat wondered why the sudden turn to domesticity. By the time she'd stumbled to her room, though, she didn't care anymore.

Kat was just glad to peel off her soggy clothes. She even donned the thick red robe her mother had suggested, pulling it tight around her. It felt good. And at least the thing wasn't pink.

She propped herself up in bed and realized she was feeling quite cozy. If Caroline wished to pamper her by serving cocoa in bed, Kat would go along with it. Maybe it would disarm the woman. She'd just rest her eyes while she thought of what questions to ask.

She woke to find her mother standing over her with the cup of cocoa in hand. She started to reach for it, but her shoulder gave an awful twinge. Indeed, her whole body was aching now. She grinned up at Caroline to show she was alright, but allowed her mother to set the mug down into her hands.

Kat tried to recall everything she'd learned tonight, and the questions Tony had. She grabbed at the memory of his parting words. She felt sure she could puzzle out something to help him, especially if she managed to worm something out of Caroline. But she'd have to be subtle.

"Verity Belue." Kat found herself blurting out.

Her mother gave a very satisfactory start. Then Caroline controlled herself. "What about the woman?"

Kat heard quite a tale in her mother's tone. "So you do know Ms. Belue?"

Caroline sat down on the edge of the bed. "I've met her." She watched as Kat began to sip her hot chocolate. "She's efficient. Not your father's type."

Kat heard the defensive note again. So Verity was nothing like Caroline and perhaps that worried her. "How long has she worked right by his side?"

Her mother shifted and stared into space. "Six or seven years now." Caroline bared her teeth in a fake smile. Obviously aware that Kat was needling her. "The woman's likely infatuated with Miles. We do seem to idolize these strong silent types, until we learn better."

Kat grinned. "And you learned better?"

Caroline reached out to place her palm on her daughter's forehead. "I think you might be running a fever."

Kat didn't want her mother to change the subject, just when it looked to be getting interesting. *If she really feels that way about Ms. Belue, why the secret meeting?* She scrutinized Caroline's face as she asked her next question. "Haven't you thought about getting together with her to discuss Dad?"

"You definitely have a fever." Her mother's face was a complete blank. Her mother, the actress.

Kat ignored that and sipped a little more of the cocoa as she wracked her brain. She needed to keep Caroline talking about this Ms. Belue. The woman could've discovered David's intrusion on her workpad, which would explain Rossiter trying to kill the kid. But that assumed she would sanction the murder of her own son—Kat had trouble with that. Still, the woman was central to what was happening, and Kat wanted to find out more about her.

"I'm fine, Mother. But you must have more to say about Ms. Belue."

Caroline sniffed. "You have to drink up all your hot chocolate. It'll help you relax."

Kat complied to keep her mother on the hook. "Okay, now spill it."

Caroline took the empty cup from her daughter and placed it on the nightstand with a sigh. "She's a nice lady."

Not the kind to order her son murdered, then? Kat wondered what really caused Rossiter to go after David. And Tony wanted to know why now. "Is that all you can say?"

Her mother ignored her. "Some things you just can't do on your own, you know. That's a lesson you still need to learn, sweetheart."

"Back to Ms. Belue—"

"I hope you don't have to learn it the hard way."

Kat started to lean forward. Then the thought occurred to her. The reason David with his amateur investigation would have to be killed was that he'd discovered too much. *Obviously.* They would have to know what he had discovered, though, somehow.

But the reason for taking the kid out *now* would be because the conspirators were ready to take action, and soon. Otherwise the investigation into David's death would threaten whatever they planned. She had to talk to Tony.

"Mother, I have to go." Kat began to get out of bed, or tried.

Caroline grabbed her daughter's shoulders and pushed her back down. "You've caught something, darling. I'm not surprised the way you run around all night, but you're not going anywhere now." Her mother removed a couple of the pillows and pushed Kat down flat on the bed. "What you're going to do is get plenty of rest. So you can recover."

Kat struggled, but Caroline held her down with ease. *Am I really that weak?* "It's urgent business. There are things I *need* to do." Kat tried to remember what she'd done with her FURCS pad. She could send Tony a message. "Find my pad."

Her mother ignored her again. "I'll take care of you. See you spend a couple days in bed."

"That's not going to happen." The prospect of days in bed alarmed Kat so much, she almost managed to lift her head off the pillow.

"We'll see." Caroline smiled sweetly. "You rest, and let others take care of everything."

"Mother," Kat protested. But she could barely get the word out.

"I'll just keep you here for the next couple days, Katherine, and then it will all be over."

Kat nestled her head into the pillow, even as her mind started to panic. *Mother, what have you done?* She couldn't seem to say anything. There had been something she wanted, needed to say, but she failed to recall.

Caroline was looking down, straight into Kat's eyes. "You're terribly headstrong. You get that from your father, you know. So I added a little something to your cocoa, to make sure you get plenty of rest. Then you'll feel much better."

In the cocoa?

"Remember, Katherine. There are some things you can't fight on your own."

Kat struggled against the deep eddies dragging her thoughts under the water, trying to make sense of what her mother was saying.

"And darling, there are some things you can't fight at all."

Kat drifted off into the dark.

Chapter 13

Conspiracy Facts

4:15 p.m. Tuesday, December 17th

DAVID felt like a new man as he stood, peaceful and calm, silent in the shade of the perimeter wall. He looked out at his crew as they wrapped up for the day. Normally the large cart would be coming soon to pick up the men, but since they'd worked around so close to the main gate, today they'd all be walking to the tram station to go home. He was pleased with their progress. Almost three weeks, but over three quarters of the buffer zone had been completed.

Both days David had been absent, Ken himself had come to supervise the crew, so of course they'd worked harder than ever. And then been glad to see David's return.

David had shown up for work this morning, not quite at the crack of dawn but early enough, feeling renewed and ready to get back to business as usual. Indeed, that's what he'd been ordered to do. Security Chief Nelson had sternly warned him not to talk with anyone about Rossiter and what had happened, or anything else pertaining to the investigation. To just go about his normal routine.

After Nelson had finished with him, David had crashed in his dorm room, getting to bed far earlier than he had for a long time. He'd woken refreshed just after dawn, ready for the day. In the bright light of morning the adventures of the previous night, of the past couple weeks, had all retreated like a dream fading. And he'd been happy to head to work.

Ken had grumbled a bit when David called him on his FURCS pad to inform his boss he would be back on the job. Ken had surely enjoyed chivvying the crew, but the man had more important matters demanding his attention, and David had nudged his boss onto those. That's when he'd found out about the change in the schedule.

The crew had advanced so close to the main gate that it would've been too inconvenient to use the east gate for all their comings and goings. But the guards wanted to maintain tighter security at the main gate. So Ken had arranged for the main gate to be opened twice, once in the morning and once in the evening.

David had the use of one of the carts and could have traveled all the way to the east gate to have his lunch inside the compound if he'd wanted, but that seemed silly. He'd brought a packed lunch like the rest of his crew. He'd enjoyed it, and the cool, fresh air and the shining sun, and even permitted himself to pitch in and do a fair bit of the work.

He'd taken it easy with his crew, too, allowing them to go slow the whole day. After all, it was more important to get the job done right, and by now his crew knew what they were doing—enough anyway that he didn't need to keep an eagle eye on them all the time.

Most of the day he'd been able to keep his mind blank, and that had been refreshing, too. But as the day wound down, David found his thoughts returning to the dilemma, the one he now shared with Lt. Henson and Chief Nelson and Officer Miles. Not to mention who else they might've told about what had been going on. It wasn't all on David anymore.

He wondered how well the lieutenant's trusted men were doing at watching his mother, if they had managed to keep her from communicating with the other conspirators. He found himself particularly curious about what Nelson might have his security staff doing. The man hadn't given him the slightest hint. But the security chief had impressed him with his methodical approach and keen mind.

David wished he could be more like that. He'd heard Nelson raise some questions with the director's daughter last night, even though the man had kept his voice low. Now his mind drifted back. *Why did Rossiter want to kill me? And why now?*

He took a long slug from his water bottle as he considered. Simple questions, but he couldn't allow himself to jump to hasty conclusions, the way he'd done often enough. He needed to go through everything he knew, everything he'd seen and heard. And rethink it all from square one.

Though he didn't have the time for that now—he needed to gather his crew and get them moving. He'd spotted the new sergeant, Carruthers, who had taken the place of the absent Sgt. Rossiter, walking over to talk to the guard detail. David hustled across to have his own word with the man.

He'd met Carruthers in the morning when the sergeant had come to set up the day's detail. But the man had been in quite a rush then and hadn't been able to answer any questions. Maybe he could now.

"Sergeant."

Carruthers stepped away from the guards and toward David, nodding. "I'm just checking to make sure these men know the routine. And you. This is a special circumstance. I want your entire crew escorted through in one tight group. We won't open back up for any stragglers, understood?"

David nodded. "Nobody's allowed to walk back over the finished ground, so anyone who's left behind would have to walk all the way to the east gate to get back in, and that's over three miles."

Carruthers shook his head. "All the other gates have been closed for the day."

David sighed. "Then I'd better work on rounding everyone up. They're already finishing, they just need to get their gear together. But first—" He felt a tiny qualm, because what he was about to ask didn't really fit with Chief Nelson's orders. "Do you know what happened to Sgt. Rossiter?"

"Good question. I probably shouldn't say anything, but—" The sergeant looked over his shoulder at the lounging guards before continuing. "It's the bloodiest mess. First, Lt. Henson relieves Sgt. Rossiter of duty, though no one knows why. Then the sergeant takes his gear and leaves the barracks in a big huff. And then this morning Colonel Gray finds out and orders some of the guards to go out looking for Rossiter and drag him back, whatever it takes. And they're still looking."

"Huh." Which was all the response David could manage. At least everyone had a reason for Rossiter's disappearance that didn't involve looking for a dead body.

Carruthers frowned. "With no sign of the man, I've had to take on some of his work, too."

David shook his head in commiseration. "Well, thanks for satisfying my curiosity. I'll do my part to help this go smoothly, and let you get back to your own job."

Carruthers nodded and went back to the guard detail, while David turned and walked over to grab a flag out of Greg's hand.

"I'll finish that." He took the spade from Greg, too. "Get your gear and start the others forming up to leave."

Greg nodded and pointed. "Another one's ready over there." Then he trotted over to the next closest crew member, presumably to spread the word that they'd best get moving.

David ran over to the base camp and grabbed a couple of the sensors to plant. As he ran back, crew members straggled past him toward the base camp to grab their things. Ready to quit the day and get some grub, no doubt. He was replacing the second piece of sod when Greg returned to give his report.

"Everyone's gathering their gear. All except for Jake and Stan."

David grinned. "Don't tell me those two continued working. Have they lost their appetites?"

Greg blushed. "Sorry. I meant I couldn't find them. Eric said they've already left for the day."

David frowned. Simply taking off work without informing their supervisor was a new low, even for those two, and just when he'd started thinking they had improved in their work habits. Maybe he'd gone too easy on them.

With the main gate having been closed all day, they must've walked all the way around to the east gate to ditch the job. Which seemed a lot of effort to avoid work. Perhaps Eric had truly reformed since he hadn't taken off with them, but someone should have told David before now.

David sighed and waved Greg on. He did a last check of his own work, and by the time he trudged back to the base camp, the entire crew had assembled. Carruthers and the two guards stood off to the side, quiet and watching.

David clapped his hands. "All right, folks. Let's not waste any time. Supper's waiting."

Then he shooed them forward. The two guards snapped to and jumped to march ahead of the crew, rifles at the ready. Carruthers dropped back to walk at the rear of the flock with David, who was there to shepherd his sheep along and make sure they didn't stray. The sergeant might have had the same idea, or he might've wanted to keep an eye on David.

Without exception, everyone hustled to get inside, and they were all trundling through the gate in no time and stampeding up the street. David's crew made straight for the tram station. The two guards sped toward their HQ, and likely the mess hall.

David lingered, looking around. In addition to the two guards closing the gate, four more stood by with their rifles, and he appreciated the extra vigilance. Since it was his work crew they opened up to let through, he felt a responsibility. He was heartened to see the guards were taking the vulnerability seriously, despite Chief Gray's apparent attitude of negligence.

He wished everyone else were a little more cognizant of the threat. This morning he'd chatted with some of his fellow students around the dorm for the first time in a long time, and it had startled him how little they seemed to be aware of danger to the compound. Even the volunteers on his work crew took the possibility of being attacked in stride, though at least they took the job itself seriously now—most of them.

David glanced around for Sgt. Carruthers, to offer him thanks, but the man had disappeared. As had everyone *but* David. He took a deep breath and began strolling up the sidewalk along the main thoroughfare. He just wanted to walk, and try to collect his thoughts.

If he was going to start with what he knew for a fact, without any doubt, then he actually needed to begin with the end. Sgt. Rossiter *had* tried to murder him. The man must have had a reason, one of his own, or if he was acting on orders, then the person who sent the sergeant after David had lent it to him. That was the why.

David himself wasn't a threat to anyone, he was sure of that. So it could only be something he knew, and not anything he'd been told, but had discovered first hand, or there wouldn't have been much point. *No point to getting rid of me.*

He was still having a difficult time accepting the fact that someone wanted him out of the way. His amateur investigation hadn't amounted to much in the end. But David had found out a few things, and he'd told a few people. If the first question was why, and the answer was because of something he knew, then the second problem was the who.

The obvious solution to that was Rossiter himself, but David had a difficult time believing that. He had seen no indication the sergeant had noticed his tail. But even if the man had cottoned on, he'd have no reason to think David had discovered anything, unless someone who knew better had told him.

David hadn't even followed Rossiter for the last week and a half.

He raised his head as he crossed a side street and continued ambling along. Straight up the main thoroughfare, thankful there was little in the way of traffic these days, though it'd be easy enough to get run over by the tram. As he kept strolling, he lost himself in his thoughts once again.

If it wasn't Rossiter acting on his own, then one of the people David had confided in must have informed the sergeant, at least, if not given the order. The most obvious person to suspect would be David's own mother. He hadn't told her what he'd seen on her workpad, but she could have discovered that herself. And he'd confided in her about everything else, except for his doubts about Crystal.

But David couldn't believe his own mom would have him killed, or even risk his life by sharing what she knew of his investigation with people who might want him dead. So he shelved that idea and considered who else he had told—his boss, Ken, and Lt. Henson—and Crystal could easily have overheard his talk with Ken on Saturday morning or his conversations with his mother.

He hadn't told Chief Nelson or Officer Miles any of it until after Rossiter had tried to murder him. So he had three suspects if he excluded his mom. David turned the idea of his mother as one of the conspirators, or even their leader, over in his mind and found it lacking. He may not have spent much time with her in the past few years, but he knew his mom. He also knew how much she'd seemed to admire Director Miles, and the idea that she'd betray her boss so thoroughly was hard to swallow. It wasn't impossible, though. He would have to settle the question by confronting her.

With that resolve, David increased his pace and realized that he'd been heading straight for the Admin Center all along. Confronting his mother went directly against the instructions from Chief Nelson, but it was what David should've done first when he discovered the evidence on her workpad. However, he had allowed his increasing paranoia to trump his better judgment.

David checked the time and saw it was still before five—his mom wouldn't have begun to think about leaving work yet. He didn't imagine it would be the best place for them to have this talk, but there *was* no good place. *Best to get it over with.*

His course was set. It was his mother, so it was his business. But he could honor the spirit of Chief Nelson's admonition at least, by *appearing* to act as normal as possible.

So David tried to continue strolling along without exhibiting the anxiety he felt. Right through the main entrance, into the elevator and up to the fifth floor lobby. It'd just turned five when he arrived, and the intern sitting at the outer desk was already packing her bag. The girl was flustered by his appearance.

"I'm sorry, the office is about to close—" She shrugged her shoulders.

David wasn't sure what that shrug was all about. "I'm Ms. Belue's son. Popping in to say hi."

The receptionist blushed. "That's fine, but. Security, you know? I'll need to see your ID."

David smiled and nodded and took his FURCS pad from his shirt pocket to show her.

"Sure." And she waved him to the door behind her and went back to putting her purse together.

He circled the desk and went back into the main suite. Toby was still at his station in an end of the day flurry of activity, with no time for anything but a wave. David nodded and continued to his mother's open office door.

His mom was sitting at her desk, forking a salad into her mouth with one hand while the fingers of the other tapped and scrolled on her workpad. She glanced up and saw her son. She continued munching her lettuce as she set aside the pad and stopped working.

David sighed as he closed the door behind him. This would be painful. "We need to talk."

"Indeed we do." She washed down the previous hunk of salad with a big gulp of water and stared at her son, waiting.

He cleared his throat. "I *know*." He stopped at that. He could've used more of his time getting here actually thinking about what he would say and how. He might mention Sgt. Rossiter's night visit, but he wasn't sure if that had been to see his mother or not. He knew precious little for certain.

"Yes?" His mom pushed her half-eaten dinner to one side and leaned back.

David took a deep breath and decided he'd start with the worst of it. "I went into your workpad and checked the recent activity logs. You've been using your special access codes to alter the restrictions on the communications system. And calling Governor Roberts."

"Certainly I have." His mother considered him for a long moment. "You know, until last night, I'd assumed it'd been Crystal messing around, trying to get into those records."

David blinked. He wasn't sure what to say next. "Crystal?" Her matter-of-fact response had thrown him. Perhaps Lt. Henson's notion of secret negotiations had some merit.

His mom went on, "I hadn't considered you, and I've had to assume that Crystal was spying on me."

"Spying for whom?"

"The governor, of course, or rather his people."

David found himself nodding. "So this *has* been official. The director's been trying for some kind of settlement? And you've been doing the talking?"

"No, David. I've been helping them prepare to take over the compound."

He almost laughed before he saw she wasn't joking. "Then when I saw Sgt. Rossiter slipping out our back door—"

His mother nodded. "He'd been there meeting me, not Crystal. He came to observe one of my conversations with Governor Roberts. So Colonel Gray could be sure of what I'd said."

David tried to keep from goggling. He was determined to finish this conversation no matter how ludicrous it became. "But what about the director?"

"Miles trusts me implicitly. As well he should." His mom was looking at him rather severely. "What we should *not* be doing is talking about this. Didn't Chief Nelson warn you last night?"

David nodded absently. He'd assumed the man would talk to the director about what was going on, but Chief Nelson must've also shared the details with David's mother. It turned everything upside down.

Her face softened. "I'd hoped you'd be showing more caution, considering what almost happened to you last night."

David gestured at the closed door. "I just came to say hi. No one will think it strange that I'm visiting my mother."

"Not if you leave now. And let me get back to my work." But she said it with a slight smile and a twinkle in her eye.

David found himself nodding again. He opened the door and called back to her, "So I'll go ahead and eat dinner without you. Again." He walked out with a wave, trying to act normal.

David avoided meeting anyone's eye as he left, because he didn't *feel* normal. He waited until he'd tramped down the stairs and out of the building and across the road before he relaxed his pretense. He wanted to stop. To just stand there while he tried to absorb the ramifications of the talk he'd just had with his mom. But that would look odd indeed.

It might take him a while to process anyway, so he just kept walking. He could go home now, where Crystal the unknown quantity might or might not be making supper. Dusk was gathering, and he'd nothing else to do.

David supposed he could head to the Guard HQ and talk to Lt. Henson, and perhaps the man would stand him dinner at the mess again. The lieutenant had been quite a help, and now knew even less than David did. Still, there was that repeated warning to not share this information with anyone, and David had already pushed his luck on that.

He felt like he owed Henson, though. He might at least let the man know there was no need to concern himself about Sgt. Rossiter anymore. Unsure what to do, he strode down the sidewalk, thinking.

There remained the problem of trust. Until he knew who he could, he'd better not do anything. He considered his suspect list again. He felt confident he could cross his mother off, and that left three on. Ken, Lt. Henson, and Crystal.

David felt almost as reluctant to suspect Ken as he had his own mother, and where he'd found seemingly incriminating evidence against his mother, his basis for doubting his boss was thin indeed. He had talked with Ken about his suspicions and what he'd found, or tried to, and Ken hadn't wanted to listen.

He hadn't been able to ask his mom why she'd thought Crystal might be a spy. He had nothing to suggest she was, but no reason to trust her, either. Neither had he any evidence against Lt. Henson, but at least he had some basis for believing the man.

David shook his head and continued toward the main gate. He could always turn around. And walking helped him think things through. He had gone over everything as he headed up to his mom's office, and it had helped.

Wait. He'd only considered the who, not the second part of Chief Nelson's question, the why now.

If Rossiter had tried to kill him because of something he knew, it would've been to prevent him from revealing it. It must be recently discovered, otherwise David might've already disclosed it. Then it'd be too late to silence him. And there was only one new thing David had found out that could qualify.

His boss, Ken, had no way of knowing. Crystal might've seen, but she couldn't know what had been found. David himself, though, had told Lt. Henson all about what he'd discovered on his mom's workpad. Then David realized something he should have seen right away. It was the timeline.

After his talk with the lieutenant, the man must have talked with Sgt. Rossiter, in order to relieve the sergeant of duty. Henson had said he'd take care of Rossiter right away. That was also his public explanation for what had happened, and it was all entirely consistent.

Indeed, David had expected the lieutenant to do just such a thing after his unburdening. But Henson was the only one of the three suspects who could've known at that point what David had just discovered. And then the lieutenant had talked to the man who would shortly thereafter attempt murder.

He'd even suggested a solution that should have prevented David from sharing his story with anyone else—a path that appealed to David's desire to protect his mother. While Henson dealt with Gray and Rossiter. Except it had been David himself who had almost been dealt with—out of the game entirely.

He felt stupid for not seeing it earlier.

What now? David was convinced, but he had no proof. It was still just a theory, nothing more than speculation, and that hadn't served him too well this far. He needed to test the theory.

David tried to imagine what Lt. Henson might be thinking. The problem was that he didn't know what instructions the man had given Rossiter, or if

Henson even knew David was still alive. Depending on what the sergeant was meant to do after the murder, the lieutenant might not miss him, if Rossiter were supposed to be lying low, for instance.

If Henson knew David lived, though, he should be worried and wondering what went wrong. *Could he really not know I'm alive?* If he hadn't found out yet, then discovering David among the living could shock the man into revealing himself. David felt his heart racing as he considered this stratagem.

He breathed deep and tried to calm down. He hesitated to act on his own again, but Chief Nelson was a busy man, working hard on this very problem, who'd be irritated with David for continuing his own line of investigation. And he didn't wish to distract the man with what could be just silly notions.

The same reasoning applied to his mother. Besides, David wanted someone who could take more direct action. He pulled out his FURCS pad and hit the directory key.

Officer Miles was Internal Security and a liaison officer with the Guards. She knew everything about David's discoveries and had been sympathetic, and she'd likely know all about how the chief's investigation was proceeding. She'd know if he was barking up the wrong tree, and what to do if he wasn't.

And David owed her since she'd saved his life. He selected her entry, only to see she was currently offline. He checked the time on the FURCS pad and saw it was just a quarter past five.

From what he'd gathered last night, she might still be at the Guard HQ, or she could be eating her supper. Either way she should be back online soon. He could send her a message.

She apparently didn't go out and patrol around the compound until after dark, and it wasn't night yet, so she should still be close enough to come help him. If this wasn't all a wild goose chase. He went ahead and sent the message and marked it urgent. He felt better right away.

Now he could go and hopefully surprise Lt. Henson, and find out if there was any substance behind his theory.

David let himself continue to stroll, relaxed and carefree. It took him another ten minutes to get to the Guard Headquarters that way, and it was getting pretty dark by that time. Officer Miles must've received his message by now.

It was getting dark enough the streetlamps had started their dim glow, and the floodlight at the gate had been turned on, glaring out into the night. *No rain.* For which David was thankful, as he'd had all the downpour he could stomach last night.

The night was so clear he could see the stars. He looked up at the heavens and took a final, deep and peaceful breath. Then he marched into the lobby.

David didn't know the name of the guard posted there, but he looked familiar. More importantly, he himself was known to the man, and so he got waved into the building without question. He knew where the lieutenant's office was, and he found the door open and the man sitting at his desk, and he strode right in without knocking or saying a word. After he'd made sure his FURCS pad was recording.

Henson glanced up, his head jerking as he saw David. The man's nostrils flared and he took a few breaths before he acknowledged David's presence with a curt nod.

David nodded in return and looked around the room. He noticed the lieutenant's gun was in a holster hanging from a coat rack next to the side wall. Not that it would do David any good.

Lt. Henson smiled and rose from his chair, coming partway around the desk and half-sitting on its corner. "You're looking good."

"I understand Sgt. Rossiter has disappeared."

Henson grinned. "You wouldn't know anything about that, would you?"

"I'd assumed you sent the man packing. To get him out of the way for a while."

The lieutenant kept grinning. "I did imagine it'd be best for Rossiter to keep out of sight."

David needed an admission. "Worried he'd be questioned? Because he was supposed to kill me?"

Henson grinned wider and scratched his nose. "Well—"

The next thing David knew, the side of his head was exploding in pain. He was flying backward and crashing into the wall. He slid down to the floor in a heap. His eyelids fluttered as he tried to think what was happening.

He gritted his teeth against the agony, looking up for the lieutenant, but he couldn't see properly. He forced himself to blink several times. His vision remained blurry, but he could make out Lt. Henson standing in the middle of the room, and he could see the gun the man was holding.

Henson held the weapon off to the side. "I bet you learned this much about gun safety. You don't point a gun at someone unless you intend shooting them. And I don't want to kill you."

"Thanks."

The lieutenant stared David in the eye, moving the barrel of the weapon to aim at him. "But I will if I have to. It would distress your mother, but while she can still be helpful, she's no longer vital."

David tried to work saliva back into his now dry mouth. He wasn't going to disillusion the man. "It wasn't Chief Gray after all? You're the traitor?"

"Who am I betraying? I work for the governor. As far as I can tell, your director isn't answerable to anyone."

David struggled to remember how long ago he'd sent that message to Officer Miles. Surely she was on her way by now.

Lt. Henson chuckled. "And Gray *is* with us. But I'm the one in charge. 'The Colonel' made quite the stalking horse, but the man wasn't bright enough to be allowed to run things."

David managed to turn his head enough to see the office door. Henson must have seen, because he walked over and glanced out. He wasn't bothering with keeping his weapon trained on David anymore, and he waved his arm out at the empty space.

The lieutenant laughed. "See, no one out there. No one to listen to us, or have heard our little fight. There are still a few people in the building, so don't cry out, or I *will* have to shoot you."

David nodded. He didn't particularly feel like getting shot. He watched Henson reach down and take the FURCS pad from David's shirt pocket with the hand that wasn't holding the gun. And the lieutenant did aim his weapon while he did that. Then he tossed the pad in the trash.

Lt. Henson then pulled out his own FURCS pad and made a call while David listened. "Mathers, get Robinson and get ready."

The lieutenant kept his gun leveled at David as he contacted someone else. "Sgt. Carruthers. I'm afraid a couple of those kids from today's work crew are missing. The Belue boy just told me they didn't come through the gate this afternoon with the rest. They're not at the dorm, and they left their FURCS pads in their rooms, so we can't ping them to see, but they could still be out in the buffer zone. Grab a couple of guards and start searching for them."

With a dawning sense of horror, David realized the compound was about to be invaded, and he had inadvertently assisted their plan. He tried to sit up straighter and let slip an involuntary moan.

Henson frowned, but lowered his gun. "It's alright. It's all over now, and you've been so helpful."

David sighed. "What about Stan and Jake?"

"Concerned? Don't be. They're just doing their part, taking care of the security fence. The forces waiting on the outside only need Carruthers to open the gate in the perimeter wall and they can roll right in and down the street. I doubt there'll even be any violence, because it will all be over with before anyone knows it's begun."

"Will it?"

Before David could even register the sound of her voice, Officer Miles had blown in like a whirlwind.

Chapter 14

A Light Night

5:50 p.m. Tuesday, December 17th

KAT drove straight in even as she spoke. Henson wasn't fool enough to try shooting as she closed. He just brought the gun he'd been holding low and to the side, swinging around to smash into her kidney. She was turning in and driving her elbow into his sternum and crashing the back of her knuckles across his descending nose at the same time, which saved her from the full impact.

She gasped and Henson stumbled. She raked her left hand down his arm and sent his gun flying. She brought her knee up to slam her shin into him, but he shifted closer, pushing her off balance and at the same time grabbing her arm and twisting.

Kat circled her arm under his, breaking his grip, while her free hand reached for a handful of papers off the desk. She dropped low, flinging those sheets up and into Henson's face as she did. While he was distracted she sprang forward, launching her shoulder through the side of his knee—and she heard the mighty whack as he slammed into the ground.

She rose through the blizzard of falling paper as her eyes flew to the form sprawled on the floor, out cold and bleeding all over the place. Then she saw the kid sitting up against the wall with a great gash on the side of his head.

Kat was having a difficult time breathing, and she had to press her hand against her hip to stand upright now. The pain in her side made her want to scream. And the boy was gaping at her like a fish.

"Officer Miles, you're hurt."

At least the kid was in good enough shape to see the obvious. "Well." She paused to breathe. "Henson *was* SAS."

"He's dead?"

Kat closely scrutinized the unmoving body that lay at her feet, the former lieutenant. She blew out a long breath and shook her head. "Don't—think—so. Not—quite."

"Save your breath." The kid tried to stand, but slipped and didn't quite make it. "But someone's got to be told. Some guards and some student workers doing something at the gate. I heard him say Robinson and Mathers. They're letting the enemy in." He glanced over at Henson. "More of them, anyway."

"Under—stood." Kat nodded. "I'm not—alone. Don't—worry." She took a deep breath and winced from the pain. "Gray?"

"Him, too, probably."

Kat searched her pocket for a zip-tie and tossed it to the kid. She inclined her head toward Henson. "Think—you—can—manage?"

"I can figure out how to use this thing, yes." He smiled at her. "It may take me a few minutes to get it done, though."

Kat looked again at Henson. "No—rush."

The boy sighed and started crawling toward the lieutenant's fallen form. Kat clutched her side and hobbled out of the room as fast as she could force herself to move.

She was trying to jog down a corridor when she met Tony at the intersection. She stood up straight when she saw him. And winced from the pain.

Tony noticed, of course. "You're hurt."

Men. Kat forced a grin. "You should see Henson."

Tony didn't grin back, he frowned. "You need to get to the clinic."

"That can wait. I survived." *Barely.* Kat had to stop and catch her breath, but she could talk better now. "Henson has been dealt with. The Belue kid's wrapping him up." She jerked her head in the direction of the lieutenant's office. "Talk to the boy."

Tony remained, frowning and watching her labored breathing. She cut in ahead of him before he could say anything else about getting medical attention. "Go get the details. Guards and others up to something at the gate. I'm headed there now."

Tony nodded with obvious reluctance. "Okay. But don't try to handle this by yourself. Find some of the other guards, ones you can trust, to take with you. That's an order." He glared at her. "And don't get in any more fights."

Kat grinned. "I'll try."

Tony ignored that. "I'll find out what I can from David and make sure help gets where it's needed." Tony started toward Henson's office, but turned to look back at Kat. "Then I'll come and find you."

She watched him go for a long moment. Then she started limping as fast as she could for the back entrance, which was the quickest way to get to the barracks—the best place to find some men to back her up. After all, Tony *had* made it an order.

She was just glad he hadn't made the part about not getting into fights a direct command.

She still had a bit of a cold, not that she even noticed now. She offered a silent thanks to Caroline, who'd forced her to get a good night's rest and then some, since Kat hadn't awakened until afternoon. It had helped, too. She'd been full of energy taking on Lt. Henson, though she no longer felt up to playing the hero.

She remembered her late and rather considerable lunch, after which she'd been inclined to follow her mother's instructions to spend the entire day in bed. Then Tony had called to fulfill his promise.

Now Kat was here, doing her part, now that she understood the full picture. A lot of it anyway. She spotted a familiar figure down a side corridor as he was coming out of the mess hall. Maybe she should have headed there instead.

"MacTierney." She blurted out his name loud as she could, but she couldn't have yelled for anything. She was thankful it wasn't necessary.

The sergeant heard and hustled over to her side. "Officer Miles?" He looked at her with concern.

Kat didn't want his solicitude. "Betrayal. At the gate." She really was breathing easier. "Are there more guards in the mess?"

MacTierney shook his head. "I'm the last. I was just cleaning up."

"The barracks then. I need more men. Come." She glared at him for a moment, then started hobbling toward the exit. The sergeant ran around her to the door and held it open for her, which earned him another glare.

MacTierney blushed and looked away, but kept holding the door open wide.

Since the look hadn't said enough, Kat barked it out as an order. "Don't wait for me. Sergeant." At least it was almost a bark. "Get a move on."

He saluted sharp, let go of the door and ran the short distance across the grass to the barracks. Kat watched him as the door swung shut ahead of her. She knew he couldn't be one of the conspirators, or he wouldn't have been eating while everything was going down. But it gratified her to see him hop to it at her command.

By the time she had half-jogged across to the barracks, the sergeant was standing in the entryway calling the men to attention—only five guards, but they would be enough. They'd have to be. Though they looked as if they'd been relaxing after a filling meal. At least, they were awful slow responding to MacTierney's orders.

Kat wasn't having any of that. She was going to bark, and loud, if it took all the breath she had left. "This—is—NOT—a—drill." That almost felt good. "I need you to hustle. So move."

She had to set a good example, so she turned to start jogging back across the grass toward the main gate. Even if hurt so much she wanted to cry. Soon the sergeant had come running after and caught up, though. Then she noticed he wasn't armed.

Kat slowed and stared over at the man. "Your rifle?"

MacTierney blushed again. "We were off duty, Mam. And Colonel Gray stopped us keeping weapons in the barracks."

Of course he did. "You have a key to the armory, Sergeant?" At his nod, Kat continued, "then hurry up and get rifles for yourself and those guards, and double-time it over to the main gate."

She was definitely breathing better now, even if her side still hurt like blue blazes. She noticed the sergeant out of the corner of her eye as he took off running, but she was focused on getting to the gate. At least the floodlights there were on and shining.

Kat could make out only one guard standing by the gate at the perimeter wall. The open gate. She slowed to a trot as she passed the small guard hut, looking in through the open door to see the light was on with no one home.

She kept on toward the gate at the fastest speed she could manage. She hadn't seen another guard, but at least the one there was standing in the breach and peering out into the night. Except the man had his rifle resting with its butt on the ground.

The guard was so focused in the other direction that Kat managed to get up close behind him before he noticed, even though she was hardly being quiet. When he did hear her, he turned slow and easy.

Kat was about to bark out a question, demanding to know where the other guards were. She cut herself off when she saw it was Robinson. The fool tried to bring up his rifle. She helped him, grabbing the stock of the gun as he lifted it, and punching the rifle into his face. The man went down in a spray of blood.

Then she heard MacTierney running up behind her and glanced back over her shoulder to see the sergeant gaping. At least he had his rifle. And now Kat had a weapon as well—she brought Robinson's rifle up to her shoulder as she caught the movement of a shadow in the corner of her eye. Someone scurried farther off into the darkness of the buffer zone. The floodlights shining onto the road didn't illuminate much more than the area right between the two gates.

Kat glanced back at MacTierney. The rest of the guards hadn't arrived yet. "Stay here. Hold the line. When the others come, have four of them cover this gate, two on either side. Make sure they're ready for trouble. Take the other one with you and follow me out into the buffer zone."

Without waiting for him to acknowledge the order, she stepped past the perimeter wall, into that darkness beyond the aura of light around the road. She wasn't going to make herself a target for whoever was out there. *She* was the hunter.

At least the security fence was closed and pad-locked. For now. Maybe they were waiting on Henson to show up and take charge.

Kat circled silently around toward the floodlight on the western side of the road, and almost stepped on someone else. One of the student workers, without a weapon. Still he swung a fist at her as soon as he saw her, and Kat cracked the butt of her rifle to the side of his head, dropping him to the ground.

She heard someone shifting in the darkness, not far from her. But she couldn't see anyone. Further away she heard the sound of running feet, and she looked to see two figures stumbling up to the fence. One of them started banging his rifle into the padlock. Soon he might figure out a better way.

She raised her rifle to her shoulder and aimed, then she heard the slight step behind her.

"Don't, my dear." She'd heard that patronizing tone before—couldn't fail to recognize Gray's voice.

Kat turned her head just enough to see the man was standing behind her with his sidearm aimed at her head. He'd probably miss. She was more irked that the oaf had managed to sneak up on her.

She was considering her options when the shot rang out and she turned to see Gray crumpled down on the ground with a hole in his head. Kat scanned the darkness and finally saw Ken Cameron walking into the light from the other side of the road.

Kat saw the handgun he was holding and almost spat. "Flying haddock, that was an incredible shot."

Her gaze flew back to the fence. Those two had ignored everything to keep working on the lock, and now one of them stuck the barrel of his rifle into it. Kat took aim again and took her shot as he did.

The padlock flew loose, and the guy who'd broken it fell in a heap. The other one pulled the chain out with a quick yank and hunkered down, pushing the gate open as he ran down the road and into the darkness. She had switched her aim to the fleeing figure, but hesitated to shoot a man in the back.

She lowered her weapon as he escaped into the night. She'd recognized him. *Mathers.*

Ken Cameron had come up to her now, his own gun held at his side. "It's okay. It's over now."

Kat turned to look him in the eye. She really did need to get some marksmanship lessons out of this man somehow. "Over?" Rossiter and Henson and Gray. Mathers and Robinson and one of the student workers. There were more than that. "What about the governor's forces waiting out there?"

Cameron gazed out into the darkness with her. "Out there, somewhere, sure. But they're not prepared to take advantage of the gate being opened."

Kat half-raised her rifle. "What do you mean?"

He kept his own weapon lowered, but she noticed his eyes were vigilant. "They didn't know."

Kat thought this man might be as infuriating as Tony. "Know what? And where'd *you* come from?"

"I came around from the east gate. Element of surprise. Nelson called and said you'd need help." Cameron looked at her. "I'll send some guys with a new padlock, though it's not much of a deterrence. Keep things secure until it's sealed up again. Better make sure there's a proper guard posted, too."

Kat nodded. She'd do what needed to be done until someone else could take over. With Gray and Henson out of the picture, she wondered who was in charge now. "What about the rest of them? There are others." At least two more, by her count.

"There may be a few more out here, yes. Stay alert. But Sgt. Carruthers and a couple other guards are going through the buffer zone, searching." He turned to look at two men as they came running up— Sgt. MacTierney and another guard. He nodded to the men and turned back to Kat. "By the way, your father made me the new chief of External Security."

Kat shifted her rifle to rest on the ground and snapped a quick salute.

"Stop that." Cameron looked behind her to the shadowy heap lying on the grass and sighed. "Didn't think I'd have to shoot my predecessor."

She took a deep breath. *Definite improvement.* "You saved my life." Though she'd likely have managed on her own. "Thank you."

Cameron grunted. "Keep a guard here until we get that padlocked. Make sure Sgt. Carruthers and his men get back in alright. Then get that main gate closed, Lieutenant Miles."

"Yes, sir." Kat started to snap another salute, but faltered. "'Lieutenant'?"

"Well, someone's got to replace Henson. I want you."

"But I don't want—"

"I don't give a bag of peanuts what you want, Lieutenant. I gave you an order."

"Yes, sir." And Kat saluted.

"Stop that. And call me 'Chief'." Cameron nodded at the saluting MacTierney and stalked through the open gate into the compound.

As Kat watched him leave, she saw Tony stride past the guardhouse in her direction. He stopped to exchange a word with his new counterpart and then came to her, grinning. "You look better."

She grinned back. "Still got a bit of a cold, boss." Though he wasn't her boss anymore. She turned to the sergeant. "You two. Slip those chains through and hang the padlock back on. It may not *be* secure, but at least they won't know from looking."

MacTierney saluted. "Yes, mam."

"Stop that. And you heard the chief. It's 'Lieutenant' now." She gestured at the fence. "After you take care of those chains, I want you both to take up position about thirty yards or so down from the gate, inside the buffer zone, one on either side. And keep a watch, just in case. Until we get everything nailed down, we're not going to take any chances."

Kat looked hard at MacTierney. "Once the new locks are in place and Carruthers has returned, get that main gate closed. Then make sure there's a full four-man guard detail on this gate, and someone on the others. I'm leaving you in charge, Sergeant."

The men hustled off. Kat turned to find Tony grinning at her like a baboon.

"You were born to command," he commented.

She snorted. "I suppose you heard?"

"Straight from the man himself. I'll hate to lose you." Tony's face went blank as he stared at her for a long moment. "But I've already got a replacement."

Kat slugged him in the shoulder. "Liar."

"Not at all. I informed young David just a little bit ago that if he wanted to become an officer trainee, I'd be glad to have him."

Kat snorted again. "It'll take a long time for that kid to be ready to replace me. But he'll do."

Tony smiled. "He could never replace you. But he'll do fine."

"Once you teach him to stop thinking too much. And how to fight." Kat looked around again. Everything seemed quiet. "So, care to fill me in on the details?" *Like what you left out this afternoon.*

Tony shrugged. "It seems a couple of the student workers stayed behind in the zone at the end of the day, while another told David they'd left early. I understand Henson used that as an excuse to get the main gate opened without the usual precautions. I imagine they thought Mathers and Robinson there would be enough to keep things looking normal, at least until the tanks rolled in."

"Tanks?" Kat looked around, but what she saw was a couple of Ken's crew showing up with chains in their arms and a couple of giant padlocks. *Better than nothing.* She watched them get started before turning back to Tony. "I don't get it."

Tony grinned. "Apparently Henson was under the delusion that a 'go signal' had been sent to Governor Roberts, who would have his reinforcements waiting just down the road—waiting for everything to be opened up for them."

"A signal Ms. Belue didn't send, of course."

"And reinforcements that no longer exist. But that's a longer story."

So Kat would have to wait even longer for the missing details. She turned to watch Ken's crew as they finished their work at the fence and hustled on back into the compound. She sighed and started limping in the same direction. Tony followed her.

She sighed. *I'm hungry.* "I guess I have to get to the clinic now and let them check me out before we can get a bite to eat." Kat stopped inside the main gate and told the guards there that MacTierney was in charge and would let them know what to do, and asked one of them to make sure there were a couple guards each at the other three gates.

Tony waited for her, and then walked alongside as she limped on. "I could carry you. And if you're not headed to the clinic, I *will* carry you."

Kat looked at Tony and considered what might have been. "I could've been *your* deputy."

"No, I don't think—" She interrupted him with an elbow, jabbing him in the ribs. "Sure you *could* have, but I think this job will suit you better."

Kat wasn't sure what he meant by that and preferred not to think about it right now. "The Belue kid okay?"

Tony nodded. "He'll probably be out of the clinic by the time you get there." He grinned. "Can't you move a little faster?"

"You'll pay for that."

"The sisters will feed us for free."

Kat grinned at him. "Have I ever thanked you?"

"I don't think so. What for?"

"For teaching me how to fight in tight corners."

Epilogue

Battening the Hatches

10:45 p.m. Sunday, December 22nd

CAROLINE watched the Belue woman taking her seat at the side of Miles' desk and noticed Tony appreciating the woman's legs. While those two might make a nice couple, she hadn't detected any chemistry between them.

Still, Verity was too young to remain a widow. Perhaps Caroline could find someone for her—the woman's adoration of Miles would never get her anywhere. Caroline was confident of that, and that Ms. Belue would need help to catch a good man.

Caroline smiled at her husband. Naturally it fell to her to get things going with an opening remark. "This is the first time we've all managed to meet, at least since *that night.* Exactly one month ago." She swept her gaze around Miles' office, until it landed on Ken. "Excuse me, Mr. Cameron." She knew the man didn't want to be addressed by his title, even if he was the new chief of the Guards. "You were unable to be here for that."

Ken grunted. "Almost didn't make it here at all. But Nelson sent me an early warning."

Miles looked pained. "I sent you a message as soon as I made the decision."

"By which time I'd already made arrangements with Fiona and the girls, packed all my things, and driven halfway here." Ken scowled at her husband. The man really was a great scowler.

Tony glanced between the two men. "I suspected what Jon would do, and didn't think a heads-up would hurt anything."

Miles sighed. "David's working out alright?"

Tony grinned. "He's been learning the ropes."

Caroline noticed Verity beaming. Of course, the woman had reason to be proud of her son, but Caroline had more reason to be proud of Katherine, who had, after all, gotten hurt saving young David's life for the *second* time. She frowned over at Tony. "I'm just glad neither of them suffered any *permanent* injuries."

Ken growled. "I just hope both of them learned a good lesson from all this—though I doubt it."

Caroline smiled sweetly at him. "And what do you mean by that?"

Tony grinned even wider. "Care, your daughter is more stubborn, self-willed, and pure bull-headed than both you and Jon put together." He looked to Miles and then back to her. "It may take more than a near-death experience to get through to her."

Caroline didn't appreciate Tony's amusement at her daughter's expense. "And yet, things would've been a great deal messier if not for her." She added, "And David, I suppose."

Tony made a feeble effort to wipe the grin off his face. "They could also have made a terrible mess of everything." He looked like he might say more, but whatever it had been, he refrained.

Miles coughed softly, peering at Tony. "I'd like to know the status of the conspirators."

"The guard Mathers escaped into the forest, and the student Eric's whereabouts remain unknown. We've got Henson and Robinson and the kid named Jake, but the rest of them are dead."

Caroline looked at him. "What about Crystal?"

Tony shook his head. "We don't know whether she was really with them or not. She admitted that Henson had asked her to keep an eye on you and Ms. Belue, but she says she thought she was doing it for the good of the community. And Henson's not talking."

Caroline glared at him. "That's not satisfactory, Tony. Am I supposed to keep her on as an intern?"

Verity interjected. "We *were* playing the roles of potential traitors. Should we blame her for believing? I've let her continue on at my house."

Caroline snorted. "I hope you don't make a habit of leaving confidential information lying around."

Ms. Belue narrowed her eyes at her. "*That* was to a purpose."

Tony cleared his throat, rather loudly, and continued, "Henson has recovered, by the way. He'd a severe concussion, and lost a lot of blood. But he's well enough to be released now."

Ken grunted. "I still don't like it." He spread his glare between Miles and Tony. "Find someplace to hold them all here, and make sure they can't cause any trouble. That's what we *should* do."

Miles shook his head. "We're not set up for any kind of long-term custody, and we don't have a system of due process yet. Those changes can be made, but they shouldn't be made in a rush. Right now, we only have the legal authority to hold people prior to turning them over to outside law enforcement."

Ken scoffed, "You think our local sheriff wants them? He's got more than he can deal with now."

Miles nodded. "But we can expel them, making them his problem, instead of ours. Unfortunate, but I still think that's the only real option."

Ken growled again. "Lawyers."

Miles looked around the room. "I think it's best we get rid of the malefactors, and start clean."

"And the ones we haven't found?" Ken again. "The ones we don't know about?"

Miles looked to Tony, who fielded that question. "There's only one, Eric, that's still unaccounted for, and he could be on the outside for all we know. But if he's here, my officers will find him. Then we can put him out."

Miles picked up the thread. "If anyone else *was* involved, there's no evidence of it." He shifted his gaze to Caroline. "Not enough." And back to Tony. "And finding that proof is your job, and I trust you'll do it well."

Tony looked grim. "I've got plenty of good officers, now. We'll take care of the bad guys."

Miles nodded. "And since this morning's operation went without a hitch, word will filter out about Governor Roberts no longer posing a threat."

Ken finally smiled. "The fool thought he'd have no problem maintaining control of the Guard, with Washington being so weak. He didn't count on the U.S. military."

Caroline looked at her husband with pride. "It wasn't Miles' use of his military contacts, prying the Guard out of the governor's hand that saved us. It was his impromptu plan, how to delay Robert's use of them while he still could that was brilliant." Especially as it had given Caroline a chance to display her acting skills. "That ploy bought us the time needed."

Miles glanced over at Verity. "Thank you, Ms. Belue, for your convincing performance."

Caroline glared at her husband.

Miles must have felt the heat, for he turned with a blushing face. "Nothing to compare with yours, of course. But *she's* not an accomplished actress."

Caroline nodded to accept the implied apology. He'd make up for it later, now that she had managed to move him back into their home. "And now? You managed to get everyone this morning?"

Miles nodded. "Thanks to the—" he started to glance at Verity but stopped himself, "efforts of our excellent administrative staff, we knew exactly who was missing and where they'd be found on a Sunday morning. Family members, too, the local ones." He looked over at Chief Cameron.

Ken continued the report. "Several reliable people, pulled from the Guards and Security. We got to everyone on the list and brought them back, and all their family members."

Caroline raised an eyebrow. "All of them? Will there be enough room?"

The efficient Ms. Belue answered her question. "We have the capacity for over ten thousand residents, without crowding anyone."

Caroline knew there were less than five thousand residents, or had been before this morning. Ms. Belue probably had an exact count. "Leaving an awful lot of room. There are so many out there—"

Miles stopped her. "Too many." He looked to Tony. "Go ahead and expel Henson and the others in the morning."

Caroline didn't care about the traitors. "What about Fiona and the girls?"

Ken shifted in his chair. "They'll be alright." He didn't look like he believed that. "We couldn't know for sure what the director would decide. Or how it would all turn out." He stared at Miles. "They're set up well at the ranch, anyway. And that's too far for the kind of quick excursion we managed this morning. At least now I've been able to call them."

Verity smiled. "I removed the restrictions this afternoon, after the chiefs had completed their operation. So everyone can start calling their families for Christmas."

Miles pressed his lips together. "Then news will be filtering out fast. I'd best share some of what I've learned, so you'll be prepared."

"News?" Caroline should've already heard.

"Losing the National Guard cost the governor a lot of support. I'm told that in the morning the state legislature will be revoking his emergency powers. They'll turn the responsibility for maintaining order back to the county sheriffs, who'll have their hands full. Particularly in the larger urban areas, now the National Guard has pulled out—back to the federal military bases around the state."

Caroline glared at her husband. "And Roberts?"

Miles shrugged. "The whole state of Florida's in limbo now. Since the secession wasn't planned out very well, the legislature's got to start picking up the pieces. Who knows how long until they can manage an election to replace the man?"

Her husband glanced around the room through his glasses. "But the secession announcement had a broader impact. No one's rushing into anything the way Roberts did, but there's been talk of leaving the union in many of the state legislatures. Some of the southern states have mentioned forming a new union, though so far it's just talk."

Miles leaned back in his chair. "Some northern states have been floating the idea of joining Canada. If the Canadians will have them. The D.C. corridor's in the worst shape of all, so Washington has plenty to do taking care of their own back yard. The biggest news is the Chinese takeover of California."

Caroline almost jumped out of her seat. "They invaded Hollywood?"

Miles smiled and waved her back into her seat. "More like a corporate takeover. You could say that California sold itself to the highest bidder."

Caroline shrugged. "Well, since someone else is picking up the tab..."

Tony rubbed his chin. "A lot's happened in the last month."

Miles nodded. "Things may deteriorate rapidly across the country. But under the circumstances, it's likely to get much worse in our area." He gave Ken a grim look.

"We're just completing the modifications to the wall and installing the new defense system. I've got to train more guards. But we'll be ready."

"Good. Because we're a safe haven. Which also makes us a target, and more of one the worse things get out there." Miles paused and smiled at Caroline.

She knew he was giving her an opportunity for a dramatic exit line. "So, we batten down the hatches and hope there's something left after the storm."

The end (for now.)

Bonus Material

The following 'deleted scene' takes place after the Prologue and prior to Chapter 1 (and contains spoilers for the rest of the book.)

Verity's Night Out

9:55 p.m. Friday, November 22nd

VERITY took a few steps down the right side aisle, scanning the crowd as she looked for a seat. Far to her left she saw Katherine Miles with a few friends— come to see her mother's one-woman performance. Verity watched them for a moment as they laughed together and made their way to seats far in the back. If she'd read Katherine right, the girl hadn't told her companions this was her mother they were about to watch. *At least Caroline gets to see her daughter.*

Banishing such regrets as futile, Verity found a seat right on the aisle and went back to scanning the people around her while the lights were still up. She wore one of the evening dresses she kept in the back of her closet. She had moussed and blow-dried her hair to give it some body and wave she didn't usually bother with. And since she was also smiling no one was likely to recognize her.

There *were* a few people who would see through this disguise, but Jon was working late as usual and Verity didn't expect to see her son here—he came to these things as rarely as she did. David was probably back at his dorm room, studying hard.

It was too bad he'd never have the chance to be the kind of lawyer he dreamed of. Everything would be changing, bringing new and different opportunities though, and she was confident her son would be able to find his way. *We'll all have to.*

She gripped the tiny silver clutch in her lap with both hands and turned her gaze to the empty stage as the lights dimmed. She expected to enjoy this as entertainment but she was also curious to see Caroline Sanderson perform. This would be Verity's first time to see the woman in action. On stage, at least.

Verity's purse began vibrating violently and she sighed. She'd only brought the thing to have something to carry her FURCS pad in because she could never leave the thing behind. Now she wished she'd left it back at the house regardless. She grinned at the thought of it buzzing away on the kitchen counter as she enjoyed the play.

She sighed again. The curtain hadn't even been raised yet. *Maybe I'll have another chance, another night.* She knew she was kidding herself.

Taking a deep breath she rose and glided up the aisle toward the exit. She made it out of the theatre before the play had started and drifted through the empty lobby and the wide doors of the Media Centre out into the crisp night air. She took a moment to gaze overhead and appreciate the clear sky and the stars twinkling. The moon hung low on the horizon, shining bright.

Lowering her gaze back to the earth, she strode across the Green—cutting as straight a line as possible through the picnicking couples, ignoring them except as obstacles to be avoided. *Back to the Admin Center.* Sometimes it seemed she lived there just as much as Jon did these days.

Approaching the back entrance, her FURCS pad synched with the security system and unlocked the door just as her hand touched the knob. She would never understand why so many insisted on doing it manually.

She strode through the back corridors around to the main elevator and waited. At this time of night it didn't take long to arrive. Of course up on the fifth floor no one was stationed at the reception desk—and the security door required more than an electronic pass.

Verity dug her security key out her purse and inserted it into the pad and pressed her thumb to the screen. She slid the key into the lock with her other hand and turned and pushed the door open. *Those boys do like their security toys.*

She stepped through into the office suite, kicking the door shut behind her and stuffing the FURCS pad and key back into her purse. She blinked as her eyes adjusted to the bright lights. Jon would surely be in his office, but no one else appeared to be there. If whatever crisis prompted him to call for her assistance required more than her, that additional help had yet to arrive. Or more probably, he'd leave it to her to summon whoever else might be needed.

She circled around Toby's square of desks in the middle of the room and made straight for the large oak door with 'FURC Director Jonathan Miles' embossed on it. If it were an emergency, she'd rather not take the time to drop her bag in her own office.

Jon's door stood slightly ajar. Pushing her way in, she found Security Chief Nelson lounging on the sofa with a plate of cheese and crackers in one hand and a cup of tea in the other. A tray with the teapot and cups and saucers and a platter full of snacks sat on the coffee table in the middle of the room.

Jon was sitting behind his desk, smiling weakly with his own cup cooling in front of him. "I just sat down, Ms. Belue, so I hope you don't mind pouring tea for yourself."

Apparently it was more of a party than an emergency. A very small party. Nelson turned his head and gaped at her as she stood there in the doorway. At least she was dressed for the occasion.

Verity threw her purse down onto one of the visitor chairs and perched on the other. "You can close your mouth, Mr. Nelson." She poured a tiny dollop of cream into the cup and slowly added some of the freshly brewed tea. *A tea party, how nice.*

As she lifted the saucer, and then the cup to her lips, she surveyed the two men's faces. Neither one looked like they had any urgent business needing to be dealt with. Jon looked weary with bags under his eyes, but there was nothing unusual about that.

Chief Nelson looked tired as well. But he simply leaned back and grinned at her—like a baboon.

Verity fixed her gaze on Jon. "I'm assuming this treatment means you're going to want me working through the night. What's the emergency?"

"Anthony just brought back a report on what's going on in Tallahassee."

That wasn't good. Of course they were rarely up to any good in the capitol these days. "Do I need to hear the full report or can you summarize it?"

"Governor Roberts has twisted all the arms he needs in order to force the legislature into voting for secession. And they'll be granting him emergency powers in the morning."

"The idiot. Or should I say idiots." Verity took another sip. At least Jon knew how to make a nice cup of tea. "That's bad enough, but I'm sure there's more. Isn't there?"

Jon dropped the forced smile. "He'll claim all federal lands and facilities for the state of Florida—including us. I'm enacting the emergency protocols so his people can't come right in and take over in the morning. But we don't have the guards or defenses to do more than slow him down if it comes to a military assault on the compound."

Verity glanced over at Anthony sprawled out on the couch and decided he deserved some rest if he'd discovered all that information. And since Jon had called her Ms. Belue, she'd better hold her tongue and let him do most of the talking.

Despite his evident weariness, there was a twinkle in Jon's eyes as he continued after her silence. "I need your help with the plan I've come up with—the one to take care of that little problem. But first we'll have to take the steps required for sealing the compound."

"I'm familiar with what needs to be done."

He rubbed the bridge of his nose and slipped his glasses back on. "Of course you are."

Chief Nelson sighed and levered himself off the sofa. "I'll let you two get on with it." He turned to Verity. "Miles has already told me what I need to do so I don't need to sit and listen to it again. And if I start now maybe I can get a nap in before morning." He flashed his gleaming teeth. "It's been a pleasure, Ms. Belue."

Verity glared at the man, but he only grinned in return and sauntered out of Jon's office. She turned back to her boss. "He must really be tired. What is it you have him doing?"

Jon glanced at the surface of the tea in his cup. "He'll be disconnecting all the hard lines in and out of the compound, except for the power cables—as long as they're willing to supply us with electricity, we'll take it. The longer we can wait to switch over to our own internal power supply, the better."

The corners of Verity's mouth twitched as she tried to refrain from laughing. "Especially since the quote unquote power supply is both highly experimental and completely untested?"

"Well, yes."

Verity shook her head. "We can go through the checklist and note who's responsible for what later. Just tell me what my part is."

"I'll want you to go up to the roof and take care of setting the security protocols on the digital communications array. And in the morning you'll need to start going through the records to compile a list of who should be inside the compound and who's away and how that corresponds to reality. And get that to Anthony so he can start his surveillance."

Verity frowned. "Surveillance? Of who?" He'd only mentioned a few of the things she'd have to do as part of activating the emergency protocols. What he hadn't gotten to yet was her part in his new plan to prevent a military assault on the compound.

Jon nodded. "You know about Chief Gray's appointment and why we suspect he's here. But since we don't know how long Roberts has been planning this move, we have to assume the man might have inserted other moles into the community. Anthony will try to keep an eye on 'the Colonel' to see if he can identify any of them."

"I see. And what about me?"

"I don't want you keeping an eye on anyone— that might compromise the acting job you'll have."

Acting? "Surely if you want an actress you'd call Caroline."

"There is a part I want her to play. But yours is a role only you can perform. Since you have the codes to access communications with the outside, and you know all the logistics of running the FURC, you'd be an invaluable asset to the enemy. And that's what I want you to become."

Verity stared at him for a long moment. "You'd have me seem to betray you."

He nodded. "People aren't aware how much we trust each other. It shouldn't be hard to sell the idea that you're overworked and underappreciated. And that you're ambitious."

She felt the corners of her mouth begin twitching again. "As long as *you* know the truth."

Jon smiled. "And Caroline will be playing the role of a bitter ex looking for opportunities to stick pins in me."

Verity shook her head. She found it ironic that the professional actress should have the part needing so little actual acting. "Perhaps I should ask her for some advice."

Jon raised his head and blinked at her before he swiveled his head to where his friend Nelson had sat a moment ago. She couldn't interpret his expression and couldn't guess what he was thinking. But since it wasn't likely to be anything like rational thought, she dismissed it.

Verity sipped her tea and neither of them said a word for several minutes. When she broke the quiet she was back to the business at hand. "I'll have to go get the checklist for the emergency protocols from my office. Then we should go over each step of the process with care. But first there are details I need to get settled about this masquerade of mine. How am I to let the governor's people know I'd be willing to betray you?"

Jon settled back in his chair. "Of course they'll assume we suspect Chief Gray, but we don't want to confirm our suspicions for them. And we certainly don't want to tip off Gray by approaching the man directly. You'll have to use your access codes to try and get to the governor. Offer yourself."

Verity nodded. "And I'll have proved my useful-
ness by reaching out when all communications are
cut off."

"If Roberts has a way to get a message to one of
his people on the inside, someone will approach
you—but we're hoping they won't have the ability.
And in that case, he'll have to steer you toward one
of his moles. Probably a low level flunky they could
afford to lose."

"Because they won't be sure if they can trust me
until I do something to earn it."

Jon nodded. Then he removed his glasses and
massaged his temple—replacing them, he looked at
her and sighed. "This could be dangerous."

"Of course it will be dangerous. But this situation is already dangerous for us all. Particularly you
and I."

Jon took a deep breath and let it exhale slowly.
"So. This is how it starts." Half a question.

Verity looked him straight in the eye. "It seems
that way. I didn't know."

About the Author

JAMES LITHERLAND is a graduate of the University of South Florida who currently resides as a Virtual Hermit in the wilds of West Tennessee.

He's lived in various places and done a number of jobs—he has been an office worker and done hard manual labor, worked (briefly) in the retail and service sectors, and he's been an instructor. Through all that, he's always been a writer.

He is a Christian who tries to walk the walk (and not talk much.)

Made in the USA
Charleston, SC
14 October 2014